The characters and events portrayed in this book are fictitious. Any similarity to real persons, living or dead is coincidental and not intended by the author.
Text copyright © 2021 Alison Golden
All rights reserved.

No part of this book may be reproduced, stored in a retrieval system, or transmitted in any form or by any means, electronic, mechanical, photocopying, recording, or otherwise, without express written permission of the publisher.

Published by Mesa Verde Publishing
P.O. Box 1002
San Carlos, CA 94070

ISBN: 979-8716429833

PRAISE FOR THE REVEREND ANNABELLE DIXON COZY MYSTERY SERIES

"Absolutely wonderful!!"
"Descriptions of even the most commonplace are beautiful."
"The best Annabelle book you've done."
"Another winner. Loved it. Can't wait for the next one."
"I couldn't put it down!"
"Best book yet, Alison. I'm not kidding. You did a heck of a job."
"I read it that night, and it was GREAT!"
"Grab it and read it, my friends."
"A real page turner and a perfect cozy mystery."
"As a former village vicar this ticks the box for me."
"I enjoyed this book from the first line to the last page."
"Annabelle, with her great intuition, caring personality, yet imperfect judgement, is a wonderful main character."
"It's fun to grab a cup of tea and pretend I'm sitting in the vicarage discussing the latest mysteries with Annabelle whilst she polishes off the last of the cupcakes."
"Great book - love Reverend Annabelle Dixon and can't wait to read more of her books."
"Annabelle reminds me of Agatha Christie's Miss Marple."

"A perfect weekend read."

"Terrific cozy mystery!"

"A wonderful read, delightful characters and if that's not enough the sinfully delicious recipes will have you coming back for more."

"Love the characters, the locations and the plots get twistier with each book."

"My own pastoral career has been pretty exciting, but I confess Annabelle has me beat!"

"This new book rocks."

"Writer has such an imagination!"

"Believable and quirky characters make it fun."

"This cozy series is a riot!"

FIREWORKS IN FRANCE

BOOKS IN THE REVEREND ANNABELLE DIXON SERIES

Chaos in Cambridge (Prequel)

Death at the Café

Murder at the Mansion

Body in the Woods

Grave in the Garage

Horror in the Highlands

Killer at the Cult

Fireworks in France

Witches at the Wedding

COLLECTIONS

Books 1-4

Death at the Café

Murder at the Mansion

Body in the Woods

Grave in the Garage

Books 5-7

Horror in the Highlands

Killer at the Cult

Fireworks in France

FIREWORKS IN FRANCE

ALISON GOLDEN

JAMIE VOUGEOT

"Some books you read. Some books you enjoy. But some books just swallow you up, heart and soul."
- Joanne Harris -

"Your emails seem to come on days when I need to read them because they are so upbeat."
- Linda W -

For a limited time, you can get the first books in each of my series - *Chaos in Cambridge, Hunted* (exclusively for subscribers - not available anywhere else), *The Case of the Screaming Beauty,* and *Mardi Gras Madness* - plus updates about new releases, promotions, and other Insider exclusives, by signing up for my mailing list at:

https://www.alisongolden.com/annabelle

NOTE

Barnet, short for "Barnet Fair," cockney rhyming slang for "hair."

CHAPTER ONE

AWAY FROM THE main routes that connected Paris, Reims, and Calais, nestled in a valley, and largely obscured by a cluster of oaks, it was mostly bad directions or lazy driving that caused visitors to discover the subtle charms of Ville d'Eauloise. Should a traveller ignore signs pointing to the glamour and bustle of far-off metro areas, and if they veered from the main road to take a narrow, rutted trail, they would find themselves descending a slope shrouded by trees, and on sunny days, dappled with light.

If they continued on, the travellers would, after a time, emerge from the forest to find a small village. From a distance, it appeared almost ramshackle. Up close, it was something quite different, however—romantic, mysterious, intriguing.

Monstrous, stone villas loomed tall. Separated by lanes and alleys, they cast shadows at all times of day. The buildings, some with turrets and crenellations, were dotted with windows, painted shutters, and flower-filled window boxes. But no detail nor decoration could hide their age.

The village was a study in history. The narrow, steeped cobblestone roads provided shortcuts, hideaways, and surprise destinations. To a local, they were practical and of little note. But to a visitor, they were enticing and exciting.

On arrival, the visitor would be drawn to *l'Église de Saint-Mathieu*, the oversized church in the centre. It dwarfed the much smaller homes, and businesses around it. It acted as a focal point for gatherings. Every small alleyway and lane led to the plaza that lay in front of the church. Local cafés, a restaurant, and stores ringed it on all sides. It was as if the village lived in supplication to God, his holiness, his spirit, his love.

But travellers rarely ignored the draw of the cities and only occasionally made the rickety journey off the main highway. For the most part, life in the village followed patterns and rhythms set in place long ago and performed with the consistency of a grandfather clock.

Inside the sombre, cavernous interior of *l'Église de Saint-Mathieu*, the stained glass windows amplified light streaming through them. The bright, mid-morning sun disseminated the jewel-toned rays on to pews, chipped stone walls, and shiny memorial plaques commemorating local lives lost in gold leaf.

Today, the medieval church was decorated further. Broad white ribbons wrapped around four pillars brightened the space. Delicate arrangements of white flowers softened the grey stone. Down the aisle, a thick, crimson carpet cloaked flagstones as jagged and irregular as the day they were laid.

The smell of melted wax filled the atmosphere. Even the crisp, spring morning air felt warm and dense inside the cool walls. An elaborately carved altar table draped in white linen stood beneath stained glass featuring pilgrims on horseback.

An infinite number of lighted candles emitted smoke upwards and provided an aura of calm. Absent the odd flicker from a candle's flame, there was silence and stillness. Everything was set. It was time.

CHAPTER TWO

VILLAGERS HAD BEGUN to gather. They took their seats quietly, giving no more than a nod here or a hushed greeting there as they tiptoed across flagstones, grateful to reach the red carpet that would muffle their footsteps. Ville d'Eauloise was a God-fearing place and attendance at Mass was sacrosanct. All the villagers would be here for this most holy of days—Easter Sunday.

Off to one side of the church, close to the altar, there was a small, brown door, low enough to cause all but the shortest of adults to duck their heads. Behind the door, Father Julien stood in front of a small mirror adjusting his vestments around his ample frame. He smoothed his hair. It was so uniformly black that it was at odds with his skin, which despite his best efforts with creams and the occasional treatment, was showing signs of age. He coughed heavily and rubbed his forehead as he struggled to regain his composure. Whether it was the change of the seasons, the challenges of getting older, or the stresses and exertions required to prepare for today's Mass, he had recently begun feeling the strains of an ageing body rather keenly. He closed his eyes and prayed that he would gather the strength to conduct the service—the most important of the Catholic year. As the senior clergyman, much was expected of him in terms of piety, devotion, and rituals. He needed a clear head, and the mild headache that was forming, bothered him.

When Father Julien opened his eyes, his gaze fell on a small envelope lying on the simple desk stood in the corner. He knew what it contained. A different but identical one had been placed under his office door every day for the past week and many weeks before that. After the second envelope arrived, he swore that he wouldn't open another, that he would discard any more that appeared, but his resolve had given way every time. And so it did again.

Father Julien roughly grabbed the envelope and tore it open, not caring whether he ruined it or its contents. As he had many times before, he pulled out the singular sheet of cheap paper he knew would be inside. He unfolded it. There, pasted to the page, was a series of letters, each one individually cut from a different source—newspaper, magazine, or book—and arranged to form a most devilish message.

YOUR TIME IS RUNNING OUT. GOD WILL NOT HELP YOU.

The priest clenched the paper between his fists, ready to tear it to shreds, but he hesitated. His headache distracted him from properly considering whether this was the right thing to do. Instead, he leant down to the small safe beneath his desk, and fishing for the key in his pocket, he opened it, struggling with the lock in his haste. After tossing the crumpled paper and its envelope inside, he slammed the safe shut with a bang.

As he straightened up, pain shot across Father Julien's shoulder. Leaning over his desk, he cast around amongst books, correspondence, and other clergy detritus until he found a pill bottle. Quickly pouring some red wine into a gold chalice, the priest popped a painkiller along with a nub of bread into his mouth. He chased them with the wine.

A few moments later, he started to feel better, and after one more brief but careful inspection of his vestments in the mirror, Father Julien left his office. He nodded at the junior priest, who stood outside his door like a guard on sentry duty and walked to the altar, his eyes roving around the sanctuary. With his back to the burgeoning congregation, he began to check that everything was in place.

The assembled villagers had been subdued before, but at the entrance of their priest, they grew even more so, calming their shuffling feet and restless bodies as they sat in silence. Many of them looked down in prayer as a group of nuns led by their Mother Superior filed along the red carpet to sit, as was customary, in the front pew that had been left empty for them. The light in the church dimmed as the big front doors were closed, and the shaft of light coming in through them was extinguished.

As Father Julien finished his pre-service checks, there was a creaking sound. The light in the church brightened briefly, there was an almighty bang from the doors, and the light in the church dimmed again. The organ stirred into life with a rousing chord. The sound reverberated around the impenetrable walls so powerfully that even the candles flickered a little.

The young woman who had rushed across the threshold was beautiful. Her glossy jet black hair framed her face and accentuated the symmetry of her features whilst her big green eyes, strong cheekbones, and neat nose were all underscored by her wide, full lips and delicate chin. A small scar peeked out from below her eyebrow. It did nothing to mar her beauty. She wore a plain white shirt punctuated by a large silver cross and a black A-line skirt with sensible shoes.

The innocence of her young features was affected only by the anxiety of her lateness. She slowed her pace and quickly trotted along the red carpet to the front pew. She slid into her seat just as the organist began in earnest. Dramatic chords rang around the cavernous space.

The interruption had distracted everyone, but now they dragged their attention back to the altar. Father Julien turned slowly, raising his arms wide to welcome his flock and envelop them in this celebration of the Resurrection of Christ. Everyone relaxed, preparing to be joyful—but only for a second. That was all it took for them to notice the strange look on Father Julien's face. His open mouth and wide eyes, the shudder of his shoulders as if he were struggling for breath, were obvious. He staggered and planted one foot forwards, swaying weakly upon it. Then, he stopped, stiffened, and fell flat on his face.

CHAPTER THREE

MIKE NICHOLLS BROUGHT out his best pair of shoes from the closet and took them to his kitchen. He laid out a newspaper, a cloth, a brush, and black polish. He poked the cloth into the polish and started to apply it. It was Annabelle's big day, and whilst not much of a churchgoer himself, he wanted to support her as best he could. As he pushed the polish into the leather, his fingers working in small circles, he thought about how his life had changed since he met the vicar.

Fifteen years of police work that put him in direct contact, and often confrontation, with the most nefarious and duplicitous of society had given Mike an emotional spectrum that was limited and distinctly dark. Anger, frustration, disappointment, and dismay came easily to him—the best he could usually hope for being the brief sense of relief he felt when justice was served. For years, he had found it impossible to smile without feeling a tinge of sadness, laughter felt bittersweet, and he had neither the time nor the inclination for silly jokes and trivial chatter. He was not a man accustomed to expressing joy.

So when he and Reverend Annabelle had begun walking their dogs on Sunday afternoons—in the hours after her morning service and before Evensong—he found it a form of therapy. It was hard to remain gruff and cynical amongst the vibrant greens and sombre browns of the Cornish countryside as the pleasing colours of summer sunsets struck them with awe. When autumn came around and the days began to shorten, it was impossible for him not to beam with genuine pleasure as the lovely vicar's cheerful laughter pealed through the still, crisp air. By the time winter's cold snaps sharpened their pace, Annabelle had become a radiant presence in the inspector's life. She was like an electrical charge crackling with positive energy and he was never more than a short glance away from her easy, comforting smile.

The concerns that plagued his thoughts—always on his work—melted away when he was with her. Her jovial manner and easy-going nature relaxed him. For the first time in years, Mike found himself smiling and laughing like the young boy he had once been. And besides, he simply could not keep a detached, apprehensive attitude when their young dogs wrestled each other so playfully around them.

Annabelle and Mike's relationship had evolved slowly and gently. Mike had come across Annabelle many times during his investigations and whilst, at first, her propensity for getting in the middle of things had irritated his sense of proper police procedure, he had quickly realised that she was marvellously talented at getting to the bottom of things. Her sense of justice—albeit from a more pious source—was as ferocious as his own, yet she managed to unearth truths and right wrongs with a delicate, sympathetic hand. It had been a revelation to him that it was possible to act on strong principles whilst feeling a deep sense of compassion. It was a lesson that made him a better detective, a better man, and a better person. Though he was loathed to admit it in these terms, Annabelle had been good for his soul.

When they had met, the inspector had been deep in the throes of a contentious divorce, losing his beloved dog in the process. Thanks to his workload and closed-off attitude, he hadn't noticed Annabelle's sincere—if somewhat clumsy—flirtations. Had one ever tickled the edges of his consciousness, he had deflected it with an angry swat. Yet, in the face of his determined grumpiness, Annabelle had been as dogged. It was she, recognising a need in him, who had convinced him to take one of the pups she had rescued—the dog he was now impossibly attached to. He had been unable to resist Molly. With her entrance into his life, warm, tender feelings, feelings that had been long buried, started to surface. His outlook turned much more optimistic. Annabelle had adopted one of Molly's brothers, and as they schooled and enjoyed their dogs together, Annabelle and Mike's relationship had matured. Now he came to think of it, as their dogs had grown, so had his and Annabelle's love for each other. Mike stopped polishing for a moment and tapped his temple. That was a profound thought, that was.

The shoes, now matte with polish, needed buffing. Mike stuck his hand inside one to get to work. He picked up a large soft brush, feeling the broad back of it against his palm as he prepared to put some effort in. He crisscrossed his shoe with quick, broad brush strokes. The leather began to shine. When he was satisfied with the gleam bouncing off the toe, he turned to the second shoe.

Mike now realised that Annabelle wasn't the enthusiastic proponent of gullible naïveté or unfounded faith that he had once thought. Rather, she was someone who held deep, sincere beliefs about the fundamental goodness in people and who, when that goodness did not readily spring forth, sought to understand instead of condemn. It was Annabelle's willingness to look beneath the surface that had helped him solve particularly difficult cases, ones that he nearly let slip through his fingers because of his cynicism and mistrust. For that, he felt deeply indebted to her professionally, but he was also wildly impressed personally. Annabelle was a formidable woman. She was loyal, intelligent, and compassionate. Once they had overcome their mutual awkwardness, they had slipped into a relationship with the kind of easy contentment that made it seem strange they had waited so long.

The shoes, now clean and shiny, sat side by side on the kitchen table, uniform and bright, the sight of them satisfying to a man like Mike, who enjoyed order and routine. He went outside to get his walking boots and threw them into his car, along with his warm jacket. He whistled for Molly, who was stretched out on her bed. She came immediately. Mike bent down to scratch her head. "Right girl, time for the best part of the week. Are you ready?" Molly gave a little bark. She was ready. They both were.

CHAPTER FOUR

INSPECTOR CHARLES BABINEAUX was, above all else, a proud man. Proud of his achievements in the police force, proud of the effort he put into his appearance—his erect frame, his carefully styled moustache, and his firm jaw. But most of all, he was proud to be French.

Pride in his home country was the reason Babineaux's three-piece suits were exclusively tailored in Paris at a cost that far exceeded what was sensible given his detective's pay. It was why he revelled in the enjoyment of distinctive national dishes—snails, mussels, and *boeuf Bourguignon*. It was why he made sure his meals were accompanied by mountains of fluffy white bread, lashings of butter, rounds of fragrant cheeses, and bottles of smoky red wine—all locally sourced, of course. His pride in his country did not stretch to car manufacturing, however. German engineering was his preference there, but when the call had come in from *l'Église de Saint-Mathieu*, the station pool had been all out of Mercedes. For his journey to Ville d'Eauloise, he had had to make do with that most iconic of French automobiles, a classic Citroen 2CV in pale baby blue.

"*Zut alors, Hugo!*" Babineaux exclaimed to the man beside him in the driver's seat, turning to him with small black eyes. They were like a bird's—sharp, observant. The inspector was in a bad mood. He had expected a quiet Sunday. A little bit of church followed by a sumptuous Easter feast that would have lasted well into the afternoon had been his plan. After that, a nap. Instead, he was now being jostled relentlessly inside a car with an infernally hard suspension on his way to a tiny village where the level of sophistication was likely to be on par with its medieval history. "We have been driving for over an hour, and there is still no sign of this Ville d'Eauloise! Are you sure this is not a prank call?" he said to his sergeant in rapid-fire French.

Sergeant Lestrange leant over the steering wheel, his sharp, beaked nose only inches from the creased map propped on the dashboard. He frowned, studying it intensely as the 2CV rattled down the road. Lestrange was younger than Babineaux, still in his thirties. He possessed the persistently uncertain, slightly-confused demeanour of a man constantly out of his depth. His lack of authority was exaggerated by the fact he wore clothes that were two sizes too big for his twig-like frame. The cuffs of his sleeves fell almost to his knuckles, whilst a belt was essential to hitch up his trousers.

"The map says it is nearby," Lestrange said. "But I can't find the road to it—there is a crease in my map!"

"This is shameful, Lestrange!" Babineaux said, slapping his thigh and leaning over. "*Incroyable!* How can it be that we, two maintainers of the law, can get lost in our own country?"

"I'm sure I have been to the village once before," Lestrange claimed. "There is a track here somewhere."

"Well, I have never heard of it, let alone visited it. It must be a wonderfully peaceful, law-abiding village to have escaped my attention through all my years of police work."

"There is a church and a convent. So I suppose it is quite a moral place, Insp . . . ."

"Stop!" cried Babineaux. Startled, Lestrange slapped his foot on the brake. The 2CV skidded forwards a full meter. "There! A track! The one we just passed!"

Lestrange wrestled the gear stick into reverse. It took him a couple of attempts and the engine whined in protest, but he backed up the car. He spun the steering wheel with more decisiveness than he was known for, and revved the engine. The 2CV set off down the bumpy dirt and gravel track that led towards the oak trees, its unforgiving suspension delivering an even more uncomfortable ride for its two occupants.

"*Oof!*" wheezed Babineaux when his head hit the roof of the car with a thump. "Drive slower, Sergeant."

"But we are *le gendarmerie*, and there has been a suspicious death of a priest! There is no time to waste!" Lestrange replied, urging the car forwards at an even more reckless pace.

"*Sacré bleu, non*! The deceased is already dead, and we cannot be of assistance if we do not arrive in one piece."

Lestrange took his foot off the accelerator, and the car immediately slowed. Babineaux narrowly avoided another head injury as the windscreen came rapidly towards him.

Lestrange winced. "Are you alright, Inspector?" he said, pushing his superior back against his seat whilst keeping his eyes on the narrow road.

"*Oui, oui!*" Babineaux said, batting with both hands at Lestrange's efforts to help him. "Get off me!" He flicked an imaginary speck from his jacket. This inexorable journey felt like it was taking hours. He would be fortunate to arrive at all.

CHAPTER FIVE

THE REST OF the drive passed in silence. They drove through the tunnel of trees to emerge to the view of Ville d'Eauloise snuggled into the valley in front of them. Babineaux finally smiled as Lestrange glided the car along a mercifully smooth stretch of road down into the valley until they reached the outskirts of the village. There, to Babineaux's dismay, they resumed their juddering journey thanks to the ancient cobblestone lanes before finally reaching the church. It had been two hours since the emergency call to their police station had been made.

When they arrived, a large crowd was gathered in the square in front of the church. The local café was doing brisk business as, distracted now from the holy nature of their day, villagers drank coffee and ate pastries to fend off the shock of Father Julien's sudden death. As they attempted to calm themselves, they gossiped and discussed what had happened to their priest. Many could not believe that the venerable Father Julien was gone even though they had witnessed his passing with their own eyes.

The Citroen 2CV skidded to a halt in their midst, almost clattering into a group of elderly, slightly shabby men who demonstrated remarkable reflexes when they hopped aside in unison. Their hatted and well-dressed womenfolk remonstrated with them, speaking loudly in French. Several attempted to smarten up their men with a tug of a lapel, or a smoothing of a jacket's shoulders, but it was mostly pointless. A group of children, bored by the adult's chatter and unconcerned about the priest's untimely death, played a hopping game on the plaza whilst their parents huddled in groups nearby.

As it rolled to a stop, everyone turned to the powder-blue vehicle. The police had arrived from the big city. A sense of anticipation in the square arose. The crowd wanted an explanation or reason for this macabre turn of events. They were looking to the occupants of this quirky car to provide it.

The doors to the car flung open. From the driver's side, a red-faced and frightened-looking man emerged. The trousers of his brown suit creased over his shoes whilst the sleeves of his jacket extended beyond his palms. His thick, chestnut hair was tousled as if he had just survived a hurricane. From the other side of the car, a tall, slim man with long limbs and olive skin climbed out carefully. In contrast to his companion, his hair was oiled and perfectly smooth. It gleamed almost as much as his shiny, expensive, heeled shoes.

The man slammed the door shut, and cast his small, dark eyes around the crowd, assessing them as if they were exotic animals. He pulled a gold pocket watch from his waistcoat, checked it with a mild shake of his head, then looked up again. He carefully drew his thumb and forefinger down the thin, sculpted moustache that sat above his top lip. The villagers looked at them warily, conducting their own assessment of these two strangers. Was this pair up to the task that lay in front of them?

"Inspector Babineaux, I presume." A voice rose above the crowd, stern and uncompromising. The villagers stepped aside to let a nun through. Babineaux bowed his head graciously as she walked up to him. After watching Babineaux, Lestrange haltingly did the same, although there seemed something more reminiscent of a curtsey about his movement.

"I am Mother Renate, Mother Superior of the Order of St. Agnès. Our convent is located at the edge of the village. As the senior religious persons of this parish, Father Julien and I knew each other quite well. Follow me." Mother Renate turned around briskly, and led the two policemen through the crowd and up the church steps.

As Babineaux and Lestrange passed through the enormous wooden doors, their eyes were drawn to the flowers, candles, and other decorations adorning the church. They seemed forlorn and jarring in light of the priest's death. Babineaux turned his head and said to Lestrange, who walked a couple of paces behind, "A most wonderfully preserved church, wouldn't you agree, Sergeant?"

Mother Renate answered before Lestrange had a chance. "I did not call you here to admire our architecture, Inspector." She stepped up to the altar and turned back to face the two police officers, the prone body of Father Julien on the floor between them. "Here he is," she growled.

They all looked down at the priest lying on the floor in his ceremonial vestments. He had been rolled over onto his back, and his mouth was slack-jawed. Colour had drained from his skin. No one had closed his eyes, and he stared at ribbons that fluttered gently from a candelabra above him.

Babineaux noticed a small man standing off to one side. The man rubbed his face with a handkerchief. He exhaled heavily. "And you are?" Babineaux asked.

The man hurried over. He offered the policeman a palm that the inspector quickly realised was sweaty. Barely squelching a look of distaste, Babineaux dropped the man's hand quickly and reached for his own handkerchief.

"Giroux, the local doctor," the man said. "I was in the congregation when Father Julien fell . . . ill.

"He *died*, Giroux," Mother Renate said. "He collapsed before he could utter a single word."

Babineaux turned his beady eyes back to the doctor. "And what do you make of this?"

"It looks like a heart attack," the doctor said in between heavy breaths. "He's a little overweight, a little arthritic, but he had no history of a heart condition. I have known Father Julien for years, as I have every person in this village. Aside from a little too much good living, he was in excellent health. This seems very . . . odd." Giroux looked at Mother Renate, presumably for support or reassurance, but her fierce eyes were fixed upon Babineaux. The doctor continued, "Which makes me think that . . . this might be due to . . . something untoward."

"He means murder, Inspector," Mother Renate said. The mother superior pursed her lips and continued to look down unflinchingly at Father Julien's body, her hands clasped in front of her.

The doctor bent down next to the priest's body and urged Babineaux to do likewise. "Look at him."

Babineaux flicked a quick glance over the dead man's face. He didn't linger there, but he noticed flecks of foam at the corners of Father Julien's mouth.

"And see his fists." Dr. Giroux indicated with his pen

the curved, contorted nature of the body's hands, fingers curled in on themselves. "If we take off his shoes, I think we'll find the same affecting his feet. See how they're pointed, the ankles stretched out? And here, look." Giroux lifted the sleeve of Father Julien's vestment to reveal a blackened patch of skin, around two inches long.

"But what is this? What does this mean?" Babineaux asked.

"These are signs of poisoning. I suspect Father Julien died of a heart attack brought on by ingesting some kind of noxious substance."

CHAPTER SIX

BABINEAUX NODDED SLOWLY, turning to make brief eye contact with Lestrange. The sergeant gazed open-mouthed at the dead body. Murder wasn't a common occurrence in this part of France, and to the inexperienced sergeant, the murder of a priest was like something from a novel.

"A murder . . ." Babineaux murmured, the glint of a sparkle in his dark eyes. "Lestrange," he barked suddenly over his shoulder, "please coordinate with the doctor here. We need a full post-mortem. Mother Superior, I would kindly ask that you provide me with the names of everyone who attended this morning's service. We shall want to interview each of them."

"There is no need, Inspector. They are already waiting for you." Mother Renate gestured down the blood-red carpet in the aisle to the open doorway of the church. Babineaux turned to look at the crowd of villagers peering inside. Unable to hear the conversation, they were desperately trying to interpret the investigator's thoughts from afar.

"There must be a couple of hundred of them," Babineaux said.

"247 in total, soon to be 249. *Madame* Moreau will have her twins soon," Mother Renate confirmed. "I'm sure you and your sergeant here can manage."

"Oh, I don't interview witnesses, Mother Superior. My skills are more . . . deductive in nature." Babineaux stroked his moustache. "But my sergeant here will be happy to oblige."

The mother superior turned to a nun, who stood at the brown door and whose arms were outstretched as she attempted to hold back the crowd. Strain etched her face. "Sister Dominique! Did you hear the inspector? Organise the villagers so that the sergeant can interview them."

The crowd behind her stirred, and a look of fear flashed across the nun's face. She redoubled her efforts to keep the crowd under control. "Yes, um, Mother Superior," she stammered as she wrestled with the swell.

"Véronique," Mother Renate called. Another nun emerged from a shadow in the corner. She was young and didn't wear a habit. "Have you found Father Raphael? I'm sure the detective would like to speak to him."

"He is not here, Mother Superior," the young woman answered. She lifted her chin.

"*What?*" hissed Mother Renate.

"We can't find him—no one knows where he is. He's not in the church, his rooms, or anywhere anyone can think of. He seems to have disappeared."

Babineaux raised a delicate eyebrow. "Who is this Father Raphael?" he asked.

"A young priest whose vocation Father Julien was overseeing," Mother Renate answered.

"Were they close?"

"I suppose," she sniffed. "He hadn't been here too long."

"Hmm." Babineaux turned and walked across the front of the altar slowly. He held one hand behind his back whilst the other stroked his moustache thoughtfully. "A priest murdered at Easter Mass . . ." he said to himself. He now waved a loose index finger as if stirring his thoughts. "In front of hundreds . . . his young apprentice fleeing the scene of the crime . . . this is not a particularly complex mystery, *is it?*"

"That is *impossible!*" a thin, high voice shouted in English. Babineaux turned to see a nun, small and blonde, standing in the office doorway. "Father Raphael would not *do* such a thing!"

"Sister Mary!" Mother Renate shouted angrily. "How dare you speak so loosely? Leave this church immediately. Return to the convent for prayer. I shall deal with you later!"

Babineaux smiled softly as he watched Sister Mary hang her head and shuffle quickly away. "It is *plausible*," he said sadly. "It is always difficult to accept a friend is capable of killing."

"Inspector," Mother Renate said sternly, "in this instance, the young woman may be impudent, but she is also correct. Father Raphael is a holy man, and it is unthinkable that he might be responsible for such a heinous act. There may well be a reasonable explanation for his disappearance. I insist that you conduct a proper investigation before making assumptions as to his character."

"Yes," Doctor Giroux added, blinking owl-like behind his rimless round glasses, "and my early assessment is only a speculation. I don't want to condemn anyone based on a superficial examination."

Babineaux spun around on his tall heels to face both of

them, the smallest hint of a smile beneath that perfect moustache.

"But of course," he insisted, "we will investigate. We will do everything we can to verify what has happened here. But I warn you—my instincts are refined and rarely incorrect. I am the best at what I do. I would be surprised if my conclusion varies greatly from my early supposition." Babineaux hummed slightly. "With all due respect, Mother Superior, persons of the cloth may be experts in forgiving wrongdoing, but they rarely have a sense for discovering it."

CHAPTER SEVEN

"SHALL WE TAKE the path through the woods?" Annabelle asked. "Or go over the hill by the lake?"

It had been a busy morning. There had been the Easter Sunday service followed by the children's Easter Egg Hunt and then one of Philippa's tremendous Sunday roasts. It would have been easy to curl up on the sofa until Evensong, but her Sunday afternoon walks with Mike and the dogs were sacrosanct. Mike pursed his lips and thought the question over as if he were considering a dessert menu.

"The lake," he asserted eventually. "I'd like to see if there are any ducks about." He waggled his elbows and pulled a face. "*Quaaack.*"

"Oh, you are a silly sort," Annabelle laughed, taking his hand and bumping into him playfully. Mike smiled and squeezed her hand in return. He whistled to call the dogs.

Things had been discreet at first for Annabelle and Mike. Many of the villagers were accustomed to seeing the inspector visit on police business. And given that Annabelle was both a pillar of the community and compelled to right wrongs in the village, it was no surprise to see him make a beeline for her each time he arrived. As their relationship had deepened, however, the inspector became an even more familiar face around the village. Rumours began. They started as whispers passed over washing lines in hushed voices along with all the other gossip of the day.

"Mrs. Markham says she saw the inspector holding the Reverend's hand at the market yesterday!"

"No!"

"I tell you it's true! And Franny said she saw him going to her cottage with a heart-shaped box of chocolates under his arm!"

"Really?"

Over time, the rumours grew more sensational, spreading like wildfire, until the state of Annabelle and Mike's relationship became one of the village's major talking points along with the proposed pedestrianisation of the village on Saturdays and whether shoppers should be charged for grocery bags.

"So what do you make of all this talk about the inspector and the vicar, Fred?"

"Load of rubbish, if you ask me!"

"Why? Vicars can have their fun like anyone else!"

"Sure... But the Reverend's not exactly the flirty type, is she? Have you seen the shoes she wears?"

Mike familiarised himself with village life. He examined every beer in every pub. He put in a heroic performance when a tea tent collapsed. He even, on Annabelle's instigation, investigated when rabbits were released after a local breeder was burgled.

The latter unleashed a wave of long-eared, grocery-eating, vegetable-stealing destruction upon the village that peaked with the ruination of the flower show at the aforementioned summer fête. Many prize blooms suffered an ignominious fate after a nighttime attack by nibbling predators. What with that, the rain, and the collapsing tea tent, the village fête was pretty disastrous that year.

Gossip among the villagers about the relationship grew ever more heated, effectively splitting Upton St. Mary in two: those who believed that the rumours were true; and those who refused to entertain them. Many believed Annabelle too lacking in the skills of romance and the inspector too scarred by his work, while others heard the sounds of wedding bells pealing loudly whenever they took a shower. But then, just as speculation reached boiling point, many of the villagers working themselves into a frenzy, one rumour away from marching up to the church and demanding an explanation, the question of whether Annabelle and Mike were a couple was settled definitively.

It happened at a birthday party for Barbara Simpson, the bubbly owner of the Dog and Duck. Annabelle and the inspector attended the packed pub, but spent much of the time engaged in conversation in one corner. This was enough, of course, to send many of the party-goers into a new tumult, but as they paused their whispers and nudges to sing "Happy Birthday" to Barbara, the diminutive, blonde, bee-hived, barnetted birthday girl, the question was settled once and for all. When Barbara bent over to blow out her candles, Annabelle and Mike exchanged a kiss. It was so tender, easy, and intimate, that every doubt was extinguished. Finally, the mystery had been solved, the entire village exhaling in unison. They could stop watching, thinking, arguing, and speculating about the question that burned so brightly in the minds of some that they were in danger of combusting, leaving nothing behind but a pile of ash.

But the calm didn't last long. After a short reprieve, the

population of Upton St. Mary switched tacks. Their interest in the relationship between their beloved vicar and her police officer beau took on a different hue. With eyes only for each other, Annabelle and the inspector couldn't explain the sudden appearance of complimentary bottles of wine during the candlelit dinners they enjoyed in local restaurants or the free tickets to performances at the village hall that were pushed under Annabelle's door. Mike would find vast bouquets of flowers, red roses predominant, abandoned on the roof of his car. Baskets of local food ("to keep your strength up") would be left on the doorstep while a neighbouring clergyman offered to take Holy Communion one Sunday ("to give you a lie-in, Annabelle.") Bemused but delighted, Annabelle and Mike accepted most of the gifts, although the baby clothes ("thought they might come in handy,") were politely returned.

The increasing warmth that greeted their relationship fuelled Annabelle and Mike's deepening intimacy. In fact, as the bluebells poked their violet flowers above the ground of the woods through which they tramped, it was the case that if there was any contention or issue in their relationship, it was that the inspector wanted something even more serious, even more dedicated, even more committed . . .

CHAPTER EIGHT

"MIKE! LOOK!" ANNABELLE called, pulling herself close against his side and pointing at a tree in the near distance. Mike leant closer to her in order to gaze where her finger pointed. "Do you see?"

He squinted and peered for a few seconds. "See what?"

"A kingfisher! There on the lower branches of that tree!"

"Ah! Yes, I see it," Mike said. "What's so special about it?"

Annabelle stood back and looked at him with a grin. "You don't know much about birds, do you?"

Mike chuckled. "I live in a city. The only birds I'm familiar with are those that flock around breadcrumbs and make a right mess. Pigeons."

Annabelle playfully slapped him on the shoulder. "Well, we shall have to fix that," she said, turning and walking off as the inspector followed. "I have just the book."

"Homework?" Mike smiled.

"Don't think of it like that," she said, threading her arm

through his as he caught up. "Think of it as another opportunity to spend some more time together."

"Bird watching?" he said. He raised his eyebrows.

"A wonderful way to spend a morning."

"If you say so."

"I do."

Mike gazed at her for a second as they walked. "You know, I can't imagine anyone else getting me to spend time on that sort of thing."

"I should hope not," quipped Annabelle.

They walked on a little further, Molly and Magic panting on either side of them. The dogs were getting tired now. But when they reached the crest of a hill beyond which a small lake glittered in the afternoon's fading light, the two dogs sprang forwards again.

Mike turned to Annabelle as she watched them run off. "You know . . ." he began. "I've taken this week off work."

"That's right, you told me. Do you have any plans?"

"Actually . . ." he said, his voice slow and steady, as if probing for the right words. "I was wondering if you might like to go somewhere. Together."

Annabelle's face froze for a second before breaking into a blush. "That sounds rather lovely. But it's short notice. And tomorrow's Easter Monday."

Mike nodded vigorously. "Of course, if you can't make it, I understand."

"No, no, let me think." Annabelle tapped her chin with her finger. "I'll have to make some arrangements."

"Uh-huh."

"And I couldn't leave until those were all set."

"Okay."

"Where did you have in mind?"

Mike inhaled. He hadn't got that far, most of his attention being focused on Annabelle's answer to his suggestion. He silently berated himself for not having thought further ahead.

"Um . . . The coast, perhaps? Brighton? Or maybe Salcombe?"

"Oh," Annabelle said, her blush fading. "That would be delightful," she added.

Mike frowned as soon as Annabelle looked away. Something wasn't quite right. He'd scored some moments with his gestures for Annabelle—he'd flown to a remote Scottish island in a helicopter, he'd given her gold earrings in the shape of the cross, and got his sister, a master baker, to create one of her extraordinary cakes with the word "*Love*" written across the top of it—but this clearly wasn't one of them. His suggestion had fallen flat in a way that his cake had not. Annabelle might have taught him a lot in their time together, but when it came to being romantic, he would have to figure that out himself.

CHAPTER NINE

BY THE TIME they were in sight of the church, rain had begun to fall. Mike took off his jacket for Annabelle to huddle beneath as they dashed up the path that led to her cottage. When they arrived at the front door, eager to get inside, Annabelle reached for the handle, only for the door to open before she could grab it. "Oh!"

"Reverend!" Philippa said, her face full of concern, the whites of her eyes showing vividly as she opened them wide. The elderly woman wiped her hands down the front of her blue apron, a habit she had developed in moments she felt most anxious. She glanced over Annabelle's shoulder. "Hello, Inspector," she said, bowing her head as if she were in the presence of royalty. The inspector eyed her carefully and nodded back not quite so regally as the two dogs scampered past Philippa to get out of the rain. She bent to catch them before they made it too far, but she was much too slow for their youth and spirits. She pursed her lips and groaned.

"What's the matter?" Annabelle asked her.

Annabelle and Philippa spent many of their days together. Having lived in Upton St. Mary all her life, Philippa was as much a pillar of the church and the local community as was Annabelle. Philippa ensured that St. Mary's bookkeeping was up-to-date, the church ran smoothly, and the various parish groups were disciplined and thriving. Leaders of vast global enterprises would be hard-pressed to out-organise Philippa. She also ensured that Annabelle was in peak condition, fortified by her delicious food, especially her cakes.

"There's someone here to see you," Philippa hissed in a low whisper, seemingly oblivious to the fact that both Annabelle and the inspector were still standing in the rain.

"Who?"

Philippa looked around, her eyes sliding from side to side. She leant in closer to say something before she suddenly changed her mind. The elderly woman stood up straight and folded her arms.

"Not someone we would expect here." Philippa pursed her lips and squinted as if she had the bitterest of oranges in her mouth.

"I'm sorry?" Annabelle asked. "Philippa, what are you on about?"

Philippa sighed and closed her eyes briefly. "She insists on speaking to you."

"Who does?" Annabelle asked again. "Who, Philippa?" She was still holding Mike's jacket over her head as raindrops dripped down her face. Mike stood behind her, fully exposed to the elements but remaining stoic in the face of them. He appeared to be doing his British best to pretend that he wasn't really being drenched by a sudden rainstorm at all.

"It's just . . ."

"Just what, Philippa?"
"She's..."
"What?"
"She's..."
"What, Philippa!"

Philippa took a deep breath. "She's *Catholic.*" Annabelle growled and looked back at Mike in apology.

"Perhaps I should go," Mike said, feeling somewhat peripheral to this inexplicable drama playing out between the two women. He was starting to get cold, and he sensed that things weren't going to resolve themselves quickly, nor would they become clearer—to him, at least. He often understood the people he arrested better than he did members of the opposite sex. At least criminals usually had a strong motive for their behaviour. Women were simply... unfathomable.

"Nonsense," Annabelle said, patting him. She shifted over and pulled him under the overhang for shelter. "I must give you that book." Annabelle turned back to Philippa. "Can we come in, please?"

"Oh!" Philippa said, standing aside.

Annabelle and the inspector hurriedly took off their coats and shoes. Philippa brought them cloths so they could mop their hair and faces.

As she handed Annabelle a towel, Philippa whispered, "I don't know what she wants. She wouldn't tell me! She's very strange. If you ask me, she might be one of those door-knockers—the ones that pretend to be all nice, and then once they've left your house, whoopsie, all your silver has gone. I mean, I wouldn't care to generalise, but I tell you, Catholics do have more than their fair share of..."

"Philippa! Will you *stop*," Annabelle said, glancing at her crossly as she slid her feet into her slippers. "I'm sure she's nothing of the sort. There's probably a completely innocent reason for her visit. Now, if you'll just let me find out what it is."

Annabelle pushed past Philippa and walked into the living room, leaving her housekeeper and the inspector standing in the hall, Mike still eyeing Philippa carefully. Neither of them spoke. Suddenly the silence was broken by a cry and then a squeal. They heard raised female voices talking over one another, chattering, laughing. There were more cries of delight. Philippa frowned. Mike relaxed. Perhaps this little drama would have a happy ending after all. He gave Philippa a sheepish smile and rocked on his heels.

Philippa, unable to contain herself, made a dash for the threshold of the living room to find out what all the fuss was about. Mike followed her. They discovered Annabelle holding a blonde, curly-haired woman by the arms as she stood back appraising her.

"Mary!" Annabelle exclaimed.

CHAPTER TEN

ANNABELLE CRUSHED THE smaller woman to her in a fierce hug and squeezed her eyes tight shut, a beatific smile on her face.

"Hello, Annabelle!" Mary said, her words muffled by the press of Annabelle's shoulder. Mary's veil was now skew-whiff and in danger of falling off. She wrapped her arms around Annabelle's waist.

"But . . . but what on earth are you doing here?" Annabelle asked.

Strangulated sounds came forth, and Mary let go of Annabelle to flail her arms around.

"What was that?"

"Annabelle, I think you're, um, suffocating her," Mike said.

"What? Oh!" Annabelle released Mary, who coughed lightly before brushing back hair that had fallen across her face. "Come, let's sit down." Annabelle led Mary to the sofa. "Philippa, Mike, this is Mary. We grew up together in London. She's my oldest friend!"

Philippa, mesmerised by the sight of an Anglican clergywoman embracing a Catholic nun, started with a jerk. Her mouth opened as her eyes flickered between the two. "Ohhhhhh," she said, releasing the sound like a puff of smoke. "In that case, I'm very sorry that I asked for proof, Sister."

Annabelle frowned at Philippa as Mary smiled awkwardly. "It's fine. I understand it's a shock turning up suddenly like this."

"Could we have some tea, Philippa?" Annabelle asked. It was not a question.

"Yes, yes, of course. I'll go put the kettle on," Philippa said, spinning around. She scurried out of the room, muttering. Annabelle wasn't paying attention, but Mike was pretty certain he heard the words, *"Barbara,"* and *"hearing about this!"* come from her lips.

"Philippa is my housekeeper and church secretary," Annabelle said, easing Mary back onto the couch and settling herself beside her. "And this is Inspector Mike," Annabelle said, waving to Mike who, still feeling surplus to requirements, was settling himself in the armchair in the corner beneath a giant aspidistra. He started to bat away leaves that kept falling in his face, an action he would soon come to realise was necessary every few seconds.

"Nice to meet you," Mary said in her delicate, fluttering voice.

"And you," Mike replied gravely.

"He's a detective," Annabelle said, flashing her eyes at him and smiling, before turning back to her friend, her eyes resting dolefully on her friend's face. "What's wrong, Mary?"

As soon as Mary had sat down, her pretty smile disappeared. She looked nervously at Annabelle with large, watery eyes. Her hands twisted in her lap. She turned them over, interlaced her fingers, stretched them out, and released them to start the cycle all over again. "I don't know who else to turn to. I . . . I had to do something, but I just didn't know who could help me." Mary buried her face in her hands before slapping them in her lap, finally managing to keep them still. "Oh, Annabelle! I don't know where to start!"

Annabelle smiled warmly, sympathetically, and Mike watched with wonder at how patient and welcoming her expression must appear to her distressed friend.

"It's alright," Annabelle said gently, picking up her old friend's warm, small hand with hers. "It's wonderful to see you—even if you do seem terribly frightened!"

Mary laughed gently and wiped her eyes with her free hand. "It's good to see you too, Annabelle. I'm sorry to spring myself on you like this. You must think me so rude."

"Of course, we don't, but, but . . . I thought you were abroad."

Mary's laugh faded into a frown. "I was, until this morning, until . . ."

Mary looked like she was about to cry so Annabelle said. "Deep breath, Mary. Why don't you tell us what's been going on? Start at the beginning, or wherever you'd like. Don't worry about how long it will take. We're not going anywhere." Mike had been planning on going home, but now realised he'd better get himself comfortable.

"You're too kind, Annabelle, Mike." Mary nodded at them both. She took a deep breath to calm herself, closing her eyes as she exhaled. After gathering her thoughts, she started to tell her story. "Six months ago, I took a break from nursing in Africa. I was feeling a—a little *unsure* about my vocation, and I needed time to contemplate, a simple life to give me the space to examine my relationship with the Almighty Father." Mary paused and shook a little. She gave

Annabelle a small smile, her eyes a startling blue against her pink cheeks.

"Go on," Annabelle urged her gently.

"St. Agnès convent in northern France is a peaceful, devout place. I've been happy there, but it hasn't been as restful as I'd hoped. When . . . when . . . *it* happened this morning, I had flashbacks to that time in London. You and me, together. Do you remember?"

"How could I forget?" Annabelle murmured. Some years earlier, before taking up her post as vicar of Upton St. Mary, her childhood friend had been framed for the deaths of two women. Annabelle had saved Mary by participating in a sting operation and unveiling the real culprit.

"I knew I had to do something, so as soon as I could, I got a lift in one of the produce trucks out of the village. I was dropped in Reims, caught the first train to Calais, a ferry to Dover, and another train to Truro."

"But how did you get from there to here? Upton St. Mary is in the middle of nowhere, and there are no buses today. It's Easter Sunday."

"Annabelle," Mary breathed. She stared at her friend, her eyes wide. "I hitched a lift! *Me.*"

CHAPTER ELEVEN

"I CAN SCARCELY believe it myself. But I—I was so confused and . . . I thought maybe . . . All I could think of was reaching you." Mary's voice gave out, and she sniffed suddenly. Not taking her eyes off her friend, Annabelle instinctively reached for a tissue from the box on the coffee table that sat there permanently for tearful situations just like this one. Well, not exactly like this one, but emotional ones which, thanks to her calling and character, Annabelle frequently experienced when her parishioners came to visit.

"Thank you," Mary said, taking the tissue and burying her nose in it. She gave a delicate toot before lifting her eyes to Annabelle again.

"So what was it that prompted you on such an urgent errand? What happened?" Annabelle prodded.

"Annabelle, Father Julien is dead! And worse, no not worse, that sounds terrible, oh I don't know . . . they suspect Father Raphael of killing him!"

Annabelle looked back at the inspector, who was listening carefully in the corner. He had found an elastic band on the sideboard and had tied the aspidistra leaves back with it. He was now sitting squarely in his armchair, his feet planted firmly on the floor, his arms lying along the sides of the chair, his hands hooked over the ends of the armrests. He reminded Annabelle of a statue she'd seen in a book, but she couldn't place it. Mike flicked his eyebrows up and down. Annabelle turned back to Mary.

"I'm not sure I know who you're talking about," Annabelle said. "Who are Fathers Julien and Raphael?"

Mary once again buried her face into her tissue and exhaled loudly but before she could speak, they were disturbed by the sound of clanging china being carried shakily into the room by Philippa. She was muttering and grumbling under her breath.

"These mutts are going to leave the house like a swamp!" Philippa said as she deposited the tray onto the coffee table with a clatter. "I'm slipping and sliding all over the place. I've half a mind to knit them some bootees before their next countryside ramble!"

"Won't you join us?" Annabelle asked as Philippa turned to leave the room, courtesy overriding her need to hear out Mary without interruption.

"Oh no, thank you. I've got to give those mongrels a good rub down." Philippa left the room, closing the door behind her a little too forcefully. Quiet descended on the room again.

Annabelle's lips formed into a little "O," and she exhaled slowly. She caught Mike's eye. He thought she looked rather attractive as she did that. She turned back towards Mary. "Please, carry on."

"My order lives in Ville d'Eauloise, a small village about eighty miles east of Paris. I, and my fellow sisters—there are thirteen of us—were attending Easter Mass at the village church along with all the villagers. There are about 250 of them."

"That's a small village."

"It is. And it is a very, very big church. Anyway, that's not important. We had just arrived and were waiting for the Mass to begin when Father Julien—he's the senior priest—he . . . he . . .," Mary took another deep breath, "he collapsed in front of the altar! Just like that. Just like the woman at the café. Dead!" Mary looked wildly around at Annabelle, then Mike. "He had his arms out wide to welcome us. We were there for the resurrection, but what we got was a crucifixion!" Mary began shredding her tissue. "They think he had a heart attack. But he was in good health, and there's talk he might have been poisoned, but that can't be! Not again!" Mary clasped Annabelle's hands and looked at her, imploring, her face pale now. "Can it?"

Annabelle squeezed Mary's hands. "I don't know, Mary, but why did this make you come to see us?"

Mary's stricken face coloured, and she briefly looked down at her lap. "Because of Father Raphael. He's the junior priest at *l'Église de Saint-Mathieu*. After Father Julien collapsed, Mother Superior called the police. The local doctor told them that he thought Father Julien might have been poisoned and when they started insinuating Father Raphael might have something to do with it, I couldn't bear to listen. That's when I got the truck to the train station, and I made my way to you."

"But why do they suspect this Father Raphael?" Mike asked, his investigative instincts taking over as he leant forwards to hear more of Mary's story.

"Because no one could find him after it happened."

"That looks pretty suspicious, don't you think?" Mike said.

"He didn't do it! Please, you must believe me," Mary pleaded with the inspector. She returned to wringing her hands as if Mike, too, had condemned the junior priest with his words. "I know he didn't! Father Raphael is a good man. He's new to the church, but he's as devout as anyone I've ever met. He's good and loving. And he adored Father Julien for his teaching and guidance. There's simply *no reason* that Raphael would kill him!"

CHAPTER TWELVE

ANNABELLE RUBBED MARY'S back as she broke down again into her tissue.

"Do the police have any other suspects?" Mike probed.

"None!" Mary said, laughing through her tears at the outrageousness of it all. "The investigation is being conducted by this awful man, an uppity detective called Inspector Babineaux. He damned Father Raphael before Father Julien's body was even cold!"

"Alright, alright, let's slow down. Perhaps you would tell us, in your own words, what happened," Mike said. "From the beginning to the end."

"Yes, Mary, do that," Annabelle said. "We'll just listen."

Mary took a shuddering breath and paused to calm herself before starting. "We had just arrived for Easter Mass. The entire village was there, of course. Father Julien was preparing for the service, one he has given many times before. It was all very routine when, just as he was about to start, and he'd opened his arms to welcome us, he pitched forwards. He landed on the carpet with a loud thump."

Mary closed her eyes to reimagine the scene. "There was this horrible sounding noise from the organist and then silence. For a few seconds, no one moved. We expected him to get up and make some reference to the resurrection. Or to say he'd tripped. Or, or . . . something. But when he didn't, Mother Superior stepped up. She's a wonderful woman—stern but fierce and righteous. Too experienced to be frozen with shock like the rest of us. She quickly made her way to Father Julien's side. She knelt down and pressed her fingers to his neck. We all waited for her to give us a sign." Mary opened her eyes. "It was horrible, Annabelle! Mother Superior raised her head and looked at us. We immediately understood what her expression meant. There was no need for words.

"After a second, people started screaming and crying. It's such a big church that the sounds echoed all around making it worse. People clutched their hands to their chests or fanned them in front of their faces. Some shielded their eyes from the sight of Father Julien's body. Some immediately knelt to pray. Others, of course, peered over their neighbour's shoulders to get a better look, and some began to inch forwards to assess the situation. But Father Julien was dead. There was no question. He was undoubtedly, indisputably dead.

"Then, Dr. Giroux came forward. He's the doctor in the village. He has seen everything. 'I am a doctor!' he called, but we all knew that. He ran up the aisle and up the steps to the altar. We craned our necks and leant forwards to watch as he knelt by Father Julien's side, desperately hoping that Mother Superior was wrong, and Dr. Giroux would announce that he was still alive. It would have been a miracle, but it was Easter Sunday, and we were *so* hopeful. The good doctor examined him. He felt for a pulse, pressed his ear to Father Julien's chest, pried open his mouth, and put a finger on his tongue to gaze inside. I could tell the situation wasn't good when he pulled a handkerchief from his pocket and dabbed at his forehead. The church is freezing even in the middle of summer.

"Then I heard Dr. Giroux tell Mother Renate—Mother Superior—that he, Father Julien, appeared to have had a heart attack. Mother Renate was displeased, but then she is often displeased. She ordered everyone out except the nuns —we were to guard the doorways to make sure no one entered the church—and she commanded me to attend to her in the sacristy."

"Why you, Mary?" Annabelle broke in gently.

Mary shrugged. "I have no idea. I am not especially in Mother Superior's favour or confidence. No one is. I was in a bit of a dither, to be honest. She made a call to the police station in Reims. 'Send an officer to *l'Église de Saint-Mathieu* in the village of Ville d'Eauloise at once!' she said, well, commanded really. 'What do you *think* has happened?' she said into the phone. That's how she is. 'There's been a death! A suspicious one!'"

"And where was Father Raphael all this time?" Mike asked.

Mary threw up her hands. Her eyes glistened. "He'd disappeared. He hasn't been seen since just before Father Julien died."

"That sounds awful," Annabelle said, handing Mary a fresh tissue before deciding to offer her the entire box.

After another bird-like toot, Mary said, "I'm so sorry to arrive out of the blue like this. I feel ridiculous sitting here and telling you about it. I know you can't do anything. This is all happening in another country, in another language, in another branch of the church. I don't know what I expected, really. I just needed to tell someone I could trust. I'm so convinced of Raphael's innocence. I'm *sure* he didn't have anything to do with Father Julien's death. Oh, I feel so helpless!"

"I'm so sorry, Mary. What a terrible thing to happen." Annabelle stroked Mary's arm as Mary shuddered and huffed next to her.

Mike looked at the two women. Between Mary's utter despair and Annabelle's slumped shoulders he saw an opportunity. It was perfect. Before his thoughts were even fully-formed, words were leaving his mouth. "I know!" Annabelle and Mary stared at him. "You can go back to France, Mary, rejoin your cloister or whatever. And Annabelle and I will go with you!"

Annabelle and Mary continued to stare at him, now united in shock. "I mean, we'll go to France, and see if we can help," Mike added.

Mary looked from him to Annabelle. "Would you really do that?"

"Well . . ." Annabelle began tentatively. "I suppose we . . ."

"We were already arranging to go *somewhere* together this week. Why don't we go to France with Mary?" Mike said, his enthusiasm for his idea gaining too much momentum to stop now. "We could take our holiday in France and, whilst we're at it, we could offer our support to the investigation—within the bounds of what the French authorities would allow, of course. Annabelle, you and I could do some digging, look around for Mary's friend whilst we enjoy the delights of the French countryside, a few glasses of wine, some great food . . ."

"And some divine pastries!" Mary cried, suddenly catching on. She beamed so brightly at Mike's suggestion that her fair skin shone. Annabelle could see her reflection in it. The vicar fixed Mike with an expression of mild amazement. "Would you?" Mary said.

There was a pause as they waited for Annabelle's response, but Mary and Mike could see her getting excited as the idea bloomed in her mind. A smile grew slowly upon her lips. "I think this could all work out quite conveniently," Annabelle said slowly. "And if there is something amiss in the accusation of this Father Raphael . . ."

"Oh, there *is,* Annabelle!" Mary insisted. "There *is.* I am absolutely positive! I would stake my life on his innocence!"

Annabelle looked from her to the inspector and back again. "Then I suppose we're going to France!"

CHAPTER THIRTEEN

ONCE THE DECISION had been made, Mary relaxed slightly. The three of them passed the time before Evensong preparing for their trip, drinking tea, and going over the details of the case.

There was a lot to do. Annabelle arranged for cover from Father Edward, an eccentric vicar from a neighbouring parish ten miles away who spent hours writing elaborate sermons which he acted out using movie references and props in front of an audience of precisely three people every Sunday. He relished the opportunity to fill in for any vicar who needed help, and had once made a sudden overnight trip to the north of Ireland to deliver his thoughts on the lessons that the movie *Avengers: Endgame* had to offer about conflicts of morality in front of an enormous (to him) congregation of twenty-four.

By six p.m. they had arranged almost everything. They'd found a dog-sitter for Molly, rescheduled the "oddly-shaped vegetable" competition, and postponed the parish council vote on whether to install a defibrillator in the red telephone box that stood on the corner of Lupin

Lane and Swineshead Road. Once that was all sorted, with the assistance of Sister Mary who seemed far too technologically savvy for someone who spent much of her time cloistered in the pious environment of a convent contemplating her vocation, they bought their ferry tickets online.

Then the phone began to ring. Continuously. Word had spread. Gossip flared across the village that Annabelle was going to France with the inspector. "Who on earth is ringing that phone off the hook?" Philippa asked as she walked into the living room with her hat on, and her coat over her arm. In her hand, she clutched a white rolled-up umbrella with a wooden handle full of knots and gnarls, a gift from woodturner William Thomas in the village. Annabelle suspected he was an admirer of Philippa's, but Philippa shushed her away when she suggested it.

"News has broken out," Mike said. He made it sound like an war announcement.

"What news?" Philippa asked.

"We're going to France!" Annabelle said, unable to conceal her excitement. "We're going to help Sister Mary with something there. Will you take care of Magic and Biscuit whilst I'm gone?"

Philippa almost dropped her brolly. "France! I'd love to go to France! They have such wonderful pastry chefs there!" she said, her eyes shining. The Eiffel Tower was almost visible in her now big, child-like eyes. Quickly she snapped back to the present. "Yes, I'll take care of things, you know I will. Just make sure you come back with lots of tales to tell. Have a lovely time, won't you? Be careful what you eat. They might slip you a snail—or even a frog's leg!" She shuddered. "And don't drink the water!"

Even Mary laughed, and whilst Annabelle would have loved to sit and chat with her old friend, it was almost time for her final service of the day. Annabelle walked Mike to the door. He pulled on his boots, drew his jacket around him, and attached Molly to her lead.

"Oh!" Annabelle exclaimed suddenly, patting Mike affectionately on the chest before marching back into the cottage. After a few moments during which Mike waited patiently on the doorstep, Annabelle re-emerged carrying a book. "I almost forgot. Your homework."

"Ah," the inspector said with a smile, taking it from her and gazing at the blue bird on the cover before sliding it carefully into his pocket. "I'll keep it for when we get back. I doubt we'll have much time for birdwatching in France."

Annabelle chuckled. "Well, we must make *some* time for ourselves whilst we're there. There's no chance I'm going to miss visiting a patisserie or two!"

"It might be difficult, what with conducting an investigation and all."

"Oh, tish! We'll have that sorted in no time."

"I hope so," Mike said. He had hopes for the trip. Big hopes.

"See you tomorrow then," Annabelle said, planting a tender kiss on the inspector's lips.

"Can't wait," Mike said. He winked at Annabelle before turning and gently tugging Molly's lead as he stepped out into the rain, his hand inside his pocket tightly gripping the small, square, velvet box that he had kept close for weeks.

CHAPTER FOURTEEN

EVEN THOUGH THE reason for their trip to France was to investigate the sudden death of a priest and the disappearance of another, Annabelle, Mike, and Mary couldn't help but feel excited as the French coast emerged on the horizon. Even Mary, who had spent much of the drive down to Dover wringing her hands, allowed herself a smile. As if pointing the way, early morning sunlight peeked through the parting clouds illuminating the comforting yellows and greens of the beach and the countryside beyond. The three of them stood on the bow of the ferry where they had stationed themselves to view the coastline. As the ferry sailed closer to Calais, if they looked past the port's containers and cranes, they could see the outline of sandstone buildings, orange-tiled roofs, and the gently undulating hills they would shortly be navigating in Annabelle's blue Mini Cooper.

To her right, Annabelle exchanged a smile with the inspector before turning slowly back to the view and extending an arm to her left around the much-smaller Mary's shoulders. It had been an awkward drive from home to the coast. Mary's concern for her missing friend had cast a gloom over the group and although Annabelle tried to jolly her along with some French jokes and terrible attempts to speak French, they mostly fell flat. Mary's anxiety was understandable, but what made things worse was Mike's equally fidgety, distracted manner. Annabelle had done her best to lift his spirits and stir up some enthusiasm but Mike had mostly gazed blankly through the windscreen, apparently lost in thought for minutes at a time.

The British weather hadn't helped. A hazy, faint dawn fought with a light drizzle for most of the drive. As the sun steadily rose, the rain showed no signs of giving up, and Annabelle called it a draw until the reality of France cast itself on the horizon. In the promising light of the early morning, the fine drizzle that had shrouded them in a mist since they left home finally stopped, and as it did so, all three of them relaxed.

"A little bit more glamorous than when we were in Scotland, wouldn't you say, Mike?" Annabelle remarked.

"In the right company, anywhere is fine by me," the inspector smiled affectionately. He briefly distracted himself from his thoughts to put his arm around Annabelle's waist. Annabelle blushed. She still found herself disarmed by Mike's affection towards her. It was lovely but strange. The clouds parted even further, and a welcome warmth crossed their faces. With Calais and the French countryside beckoning, they made their way back to the car parked in the ferry's hold.

Mike walked around to the driver's side, but before he could reach for the door handle, Annabelle clasped his wrist. "What are you doing?" she said.

"I'm going to drive," the inspector replied casually. "You

drove us down to Dover. It seems only fair that I drive the second half of the trip."

"Oh no!" Annabelle asserted, shaking her head. "No, no, no. I've never driven in France before—do you think I would give up that opportunity?"

Mike glanced at Mary, who stood on the other side of the car, pretending to look at something in the distance. "Okay then, just remember that they drive on the right here," he said as he retreated to the other side. He didn't really like being a passenger, but he had learnt not to come between Annabelle and her steering wheel when she insisted.

Soon they were driving along the autoroute out of Calais and into the countryside to the east. As quickly as she could, Annabelle turned off the autoroute to travel more leisurely through quaint towns and villages, slightly regretting her decision to drive as she focused on the road whilst Mike looked out at the view. At a traffic light, she turned on the radio and pressed the buttons until a gentle, acoustic guitar-strummed song emerged from the static.

"Ah!" she said. "French is such a beautiful language, isn't it, Mike?"

"Hmph," Mike grunted. He continued to stare out of the window.

If Mike had been a little agitated on the drive down to Dover, he was growing positively uncomfortable as they drove through France. The inspector was a sure man, confident, sceptical, and very rarely surprised. He had seen a lot in his time on the police force, and all of it had taught him what to expect and what to do. There was rarely a situation in which he felt he couldn't draw upon his previous experience.

But that was in England, and as the small Mini Cooper

whipped through France on the wrong side of the road with signs that seemed impossible to pronounce, an unknown, unintelligible singer on the radio, and an unfamiliar landscape around him, it occurred to Mike how much of his confidence stemmed from his environment. He wrapped his hand around the furry box in his pocket. He was in foreign territory.

"He's singing about a girl," Sister Mary said, poking her head between the front seats, "about how he likes her too much to tell her."

"Oh!" Annabelle exclaimed with delight, turning to Mike. "Isn't that romantic?"

"Hmph," he grunted once again.

After almost two hours of driving and with sharp, on-point directions from Mary, they found themselves on a bumpy, poorly maintained road that led between a mass of oak trees. When they emerged from the woods, Ville d'Eauloise appeared in front of them, just like it did for every visitor, settled comfortably in the valley, slate-covered turrets soaring above pointed roofs that jutted into the bright blue sky.

A sense of awe filled the small car. There was no need for Mary to direct Annabelle any further as the road down the hill and into the village led directly to the enormous, looming church at the village's centre. "Whee!" Annabelle cried as they glided down the incline.

As she drove along the cobbled streets, they became acutely aware of the onlookers who turned their heads to stare at the unfamiliar blue Mini with white go-faster stripes. They passed an elderly woman carrying a wicker basket full of laundry on her head. Another man, just as old and wizened, rode a bike with a cage of chickens strapped to the back. Children playing in the streets with a bat and ball waved as they drove by, curious about the new arrivals and excitedly pointing at the unfamiliar car.

Once they reached the large plaza in front of the church, patrons of the café, shops, and businesses gazed at them. Some paused as they brought their coffee cups halfway to their lips. Others placed their heavy shopping bags on the ground as the Mini passed by. The looks grew more intense as the trio got out. Coffee drinkers sat up in their chairs. Shoppers pulled down their sunglasses. One young child ran up to them and pointed. It was understandable. It's not every day you see a Catholic nun, an Anglican vicar, and a British police inspector step out of a small car with foreign number plates in a remote French village whilst going about your daily business. All before ten a.m.

CHAPTER FIFTEEN

"WAIT HERE," SISTER Mary said. "I shall fetch Mother Superior and Inspector Babineaux. I've arranged to meet them here."

Annabelle nodded and walked around the car to join Mike, who felt distinctly overdressed in his customary trench coat. He was self-conscious now that the sun had warmed up and the focus of the village was upon him. They watched Sister Mary walk quickly up the steps to the enormous church. There was a French police car parked close by.

"Isn't this wonderful?" Annabelle said, paying the bystanders no mind as she spun around, wide-eyed, to take in the view. "It's like being transported back to the fifteenth century!"

"I suppose," the inspector murmured, glancing sideways at the people chattering to each other whilst nodding at them. He looked up at the church. Gargoyles and eerie ugly creatures carved into the stone walls peered down at him.

Annabelle stopped spinning and faced him, hands on

hips, her lips pursed. "What on earth is the matter with you?" she said. "You've been acting strangely ever since we left home!"

Mike looked at her sharply as if he'd suddenly woken up. "Oh . . . um . . . I'm just concerned about the murder if, indeed, it is one. Police instincts, you know. Difficult for me to relax when there's an investigation in the offing."

Annabelle smiled and stepped closer. "Well, I suppose we'll just have to sort it all out as quickly as possible then." She put her arm through his and leant in for a kiss, causing a frisson of interest amongst the patrons at Café Sylvie a few yards from where they were standing.

A second later they were interrupted by the sound of footsteps pounding across the cobblestones. The tall figure of a nun bore down on them, briskly walking at a near jogging pace with a long, stiff stride, her arms pumping. Following close behind trotted a much smaller, much more flexible Sister Mary, and behind her, a well-dressed, tall, thin man strolled. His hair was glossy in the sunlight, and his gait even and steady as he concerned himself with keeping his shoulders back and his chin up.

"Annabelle, Inspector Mike, this is the Mother Superior of St. Agnès, Mother Renate," Mary said, racing to catch up as the elderly nun stopped abruptly before them. Mother Renate clasped her hands in front of her, the swaying crucifix that hung from her neck slowly coming to a halt. She offered only a stern, unsmiling expression and a quick nod as a greeting. "And this is Inspector Babineaux—he's conducting the investigation into Father Julien's death," Mary added.

"A pleasure, *madame*," Babineaux said in English, offering his hand to Annabelle.

"Reverend Dixon is a priest in England," Mary added

quickly, seeming a little alarmed at the French detective's behaviour.

Babineaux's eyes widened fractionally at this information, and he ducked his head in acknowledgement. "Indeed?"

Annabelle accepted his hand and giggled in surprise when the tall, languid man gently pulled her fingers to his lips and planted a soft kiss on the back of them, his eyes never leaving hers. "Oh!" she said.

"Sister Mary told us zat we would be joined by a couple of England's finest detectives," Babineaux said. He cast his eyes from Annabelle to the inspector, shaking Mike's hand a little more vigorously and to Mike's great relief making no attempt to kiss it. "We 'ave an interesting challenge."

"We're here on a break," Mike said. Mike made sure to grip the Frenchman's hand tightly for a couple of seconds longer than was necessary. "A holiday."

Babineaux raised a tweezed eyebrow as he looked them over. "Reverend Marple and Inspector 'olmes—it iz an interesting romance."

Annabelle giggled again. Even the policemen here were different! "Oh, I'm not a detective," she said, almost apologetically. "I'm just a friend of Mary's."

"Then why are you here?" Mother Renate cut in, almost angrily. Like Annabelle, the Mother Superior was tall. They looked each other directly in the eye. "We were told you have come to help."

"Mother Superior . . ." Mary began.

"We're here to enjoy the hospitality of your village," Mike said, suddenly feeling the urge to assert some authority. "We won't interfere with your investigation at all. But if you require our help, we'll be happy to assist." The Mother

Superior eyed Mike keenly as if ascertaining whether his assertion was well-intentioned.

Babineaux had no such qualms. "*Absolument!*" he said, tilting his head theatrically. "I would welcome ze prospect of seeing what my British counterparts 'ave to offer. Maybe we can learn from ze other."

"Very good," Mike said formally. Mary, standing outside the Mother Superior's line of sight, beamed.

"I suppose you should come in then," Mother Renate said, the words flying from her mouth as quick and hard as bullets. "We will explain what happened."

She spun on her heels and began walking back to the church with no indication that she expected them to do anything other than follow. Sister Mary quickly bowed her head and chased after Mother Renate. A second later, Mike did likewise but not before realising that Annabelle and Inspector Babineaux were walking side by side in front of him. The French detective's hands were behind his back as if they were out for a stroll rather than embarking on an investigation into a suspicious death. Mike scurried behind them, his frown deepening when he heard Annabelle giggle yet again.

Mike was so flustered that he nearly missed noticing the truck that was parked outside the café, its rear doors open to reveal trays full of bread. A nun flicked her skirts aside and clambered inside the truck. She handed a tray of loaves to the café owner, who stood waiting patiently. Several others formed a line behind him.

"What's happening over there?" Mike called out to the others ahead of him.

"Our convent makes bread," Mother Renate said after stopping and turning to see what he was looking at, "and has done for over one hundred and fifty years. St. Agnès is situated outside the village. We have fields where we grow wheat, a mill where we grind it into flour, and a bakery from which we supply the whole village and all those as far as Reims."

"It iz a wonderful bread," Babineaux called over his shoulder, "I 'ad some this morning, so soft—'ow do you say it, melt in ze mowff. Ze taste, texture iz very refined—if you 'ave ze palate for such zings." He looked at Annabelle as he said these last words, and Mike almost lost his train of thought when he saw her blush for apparently no reason at all.

CHAPTER SIXTEEN

ONCE ANNABELLE AND Mike were inside the church, Babineaux embarked on a dramatic retelling of the previous day's events. As he did so, Mother Renate tightened her lips even further, only opening them when necessary to correct salient details that the French inspector embellished in his attempt to make Father Julien's death appear as interesting as possible to their international visitors.

". . . at which point I made my wise deduction," Babineaux concluded, swiping the air with an exaggerated gesture, "zat zis was murder! And zat Father Raphael was ze killer! Ze only question is . . ." he said, pausing for effect. He leant in, staring at them. "*Why?*"

"No!" Sister Mary cried, her eyes pleading. "You're wrong! He's innocent! Father Raphael is innocent!"

Mother Renate frowned. "Sister Mary, please!" She turned to Annabelle. "I don't approve of histrionics. They are unbecoming and undignified. Please excuse Sister Mary."

"It's quite alright, Mother Superior. I have known Mary a long time, and I know how much she believes in truth and justice. If she feels so strongly, there must be a good reason."

"What do you know about the two men?" Mike asked.

"Ze Father was a priest who 'ad been 'ere for nearly twenty years. He rarely left ze village. What zere is to know, we all know. Ze junior father, 'e arrived eighteen months ago. What did 'e do before? 'e lived a regular young man's life. Apparently 'e was a model before attending seminary and being assigned to Father Julien for mentorship. 'e graced ze catwalks of gay Paree."

Mother Renate harrumphed at this piece of information. Seeing that Mary was about to protest again, Annabelle jumped in quickly, "Right, well, do you mind if we take a little look around?"

"But of course!" Babineaux said, raising his chin and standing to attention. He gestured with his arm across the expanse of the large church like he were a ringmaster at the circus.

"You may," Mother Renate said. She glared at Babineaux. Murder investigation or not, permission for their visitors to tour the church was not his to give.

Slowly, Annabelle and Mike began to wander around. Acutely aware of their hosts' watchful gazes, they whispered softly to each other.

"What do you think?" Annabelle hissed, glancing back at Mother Renate, Babineaux, and Mary. Sergeant Lestrange had joined them. They stood as if awaiting a ceremonial visit from a local dignitary.

"I've never seen a detective relish talking about a case so much—you'd think he *wanted* it to be murder!" Mike said, offering a placating smile at the line-up in the distance.

"Ridiculous way to conduct an investigation. And talk about jumping to conclusions!"

Annabelle widened her eyes and raised her eyebrows a little at this last statement. "Really? I don't know any detectives who might do that, do you?"

Mike looked back at her, his eyes narrowing. Annabelle meant something but he wasn't quite sure what. She did that sometimes.

"But no, you're right, jumping to conclusions simply won't do, will it?" she added.

There was a clang, then a bang, followed by the sound of a rush of water. A nun came out of a side door, wiping her hands. When she saw the pair, she blushed and ran away giggling.

They stepped up to the altar and looked down at the spot where Father Julien had collapsed.

"Are you sure he died from a heart attack?" Mike called across the pews.

"Yes, the doctor has confirmed it," Mother Renate said.

"But couldn't his death simply be the result of natural causes?" Annabelle asked.

"Zer is no 'istory! 'e was perfectly fine until 'e died!" Babineaux countered. "We are awaiting ze results of ze post-mortem. But it looks very, 'ow do you say, *fishy*. 'e was tortured."

"*Contorted*," Mother Renate corrected.

After examining around, on top, and behind the altar, Annabelle and the inspector found themselves at a small door. "Allow me," Babineaux said, suddenly springing to their side and opening it for them.

"Ah, his office," Annabelle said. "It is very similar to my own."

"You've seen a few of these in your time. What do you make of this one?" Mike asked.

"It's on the sparse side," Annabelle said, taking it in slowly, "but nothing out of the ordinary."

Mike strode over to the desk and tapped his foot against a safe that sat on the floor. "What's in the safe?"

CHAPTER SEVENTEEN

BABINEAUX SHRUGGED. "WHO knows?"
"You haven't opened it?" Mike frowned.
"A man's private affairs are private—even after 'is death."

Mike breathed in deeply. "But according to you, this is a murder inquiry. There may be items pertinent, if not *central* to the investigation in here."

"Father Julien was ze victim—not ze murderer. A Frenchman is entitled to 'is privacy. It may be all 'e 'as."

Mike spoke again. "And I'm sure if it *were* murder, the murderer would be just as keen to keep such things private. Look, so far, you have nothing, only conjecture. No motive or apparent understanding of the lives of either Father Julien or Father Raphael. You need all the information you can get. You can't condemn a man without knowing everything you can. You're putting the cart before the horse."

Babineaux squinted, his beady, black eyes getting beadier and blacker, a challenging look appearing on his long, slim face for the first time. He didn't exactly understand what the inspector was saying, but he suspected that the English policeman wasn't in awe of his deductive reasoning.

"Why don't we allow ze *révérend* to decide," he said, turning slowly to Annabelle. "Should we examine ze inner workings of ze man's life? Should we unveil 'is secrets, 'is little *peccadilles* to ze world? Should we . . . expose 'is inner soul, hmm?"

With both men staring at her expectantly, Annabelle gulped and considered the problem. She could see both sides and hated to pry, but she couldn't help feeling that they needed to know more.

"I know that under normal circumstances, it would be considered terribly inappropriate, but on this occasion, I do think Inspector Nicholls is right," she said. Mike grinned broadly at this before catching Annabelle's eye and quickly rearranging his features into a more serious expression. "We should try to learn as much as we can about Father Julien *and* Father Raphael, and I think opening this safe would help. It can't be difficult. It has a lock. Just needs a key."

"Very well," Babineaux said, haughtily tilting his head as he conceded defeat before walking to the open doorway. "Lestrange!" he called out loudly. He barked some instructions in French, causing the hapless sergeant to run out of the church so quickly, his footsteps echoed around the enormous interior long after he had left.

Annabelle and Mike continued to poke and peer around the small, stone-walled room for a few moments longer. They opened cupboards and scanned desk drawers mostly filled with writing equipment, paper, communion supplies, and boxes of candles.

"Par for the course," Annabelle said. "There's nothing unusual here except for how tidy it is." They returned to the sanctuary.

Mother Renate stood still as if she were built of the same stone as the walls around them. She had watched them poke around whilst Mary shifted anxiously from foot to foot, wringing her hands. Babineaux sat down, crossed his long legs, and draped his arm nonchalantly over the end of a pew. He appeared indifferent.

"Well," Babineaux said, "what iz your conclusion?"

Mike answered curtly, "Our *conclusion* is still a long way off. There is much more to do, to *investigate*."

"Would it be possible to talk to your sisters?" Annabelle asked Mother Superior.

"The sisters?" Mother Renate said incredulously, her hard emerald eyes glinting like rocks. "Why would you speak to my nuns? This is a matter of priests!"

"Yes," Mike said, "but one of them is dead, and the other has disappeared. And your sisters were there when that happened."

Mother Renate pursed her lips whilst she thought about this. "Very well. Shall I fetch them?"

"No," Annabelle answered quickly, glancing at Mike, "we've just arrived, and we would like to find somewhere to stay and settle in. Tomorrow, perhaps, once we've got the lay of the land. For now, maybe we can retire to our rooms and have a think."

Mother Renate paused before bowing her head, acceding to Annabelle's request. "We will see you tomorrow, then."

"Allow me to walk you to your car," Babineaux said, stepping forwards and offering his arm.

"You are most kind, Inspector." Annabelle accepted Babineaux's offer, and they left the church, trotting down the steps to her car. Mike and Mary walked behind.

"Ze Mini Cooper. Quite an interesting car. Very 1960s,

Carnaby Street. Mini skirts. 'ot pants. I take it, *Révérend*, zat you are as proud of your nation as I am of mine."

Annabelle chuckled. "Oh, I just like the way it looks. And small cars are easier to park."

Babineaux smiled as if this was the wisest thing ever said. "Indeed, *Révérend*."

Mike huffed a little as he made his way to his side of the car before seeing his French counterpart graciously open the driver's door for Annabelle. She smiled broadly and blushed once again whilst Mike grumbled to himself, irritated that he had never considered doing that. He tried to make up for it by opening the passenger door for Sister Mary, but it wasn't quite the same.

"If you need anyzing, please call. 'ere is my card. I am staying in ze village whilst we conduct ze investigation. *Au revoir*." Babineaux closed the car door with a click.

"That Inspector Babineaux is such a gentleman!" Annabelle said. She turned the engine on with one hand and waved at Babineaux with the other.

"Hmph," Mike grunted. "Incompetent, too."

"Can we give you a lift back to the convent?" Annabelle asked Mary's reflection in her rear view mirror.

"No, it's alright, Annabelle. I have arranged for you to stay at an auberge a few minutes away. Drop me off there, and I'll walk. It's not far."

"Very well. A guesthouse in a lovely picturesque French village. I can't wait!"

CHAPTER EIGHTEEN

FROM THE BACK seat of the car, Mary guided them to a beautiful, old villa with a lichen-covered roof. Thick vines curled their green fingers across the stonework as if comforting the squat, two-storey building. Up close, they could see buds of wisteria hanging from the green leaves like bunches of tiny purple grapes. The buds would wait for the warmer weather to arrive before opening to reveal long fronds of lilac flowers. Embedded in the walls of the building, large windows sat behind boxes full of small spring flowers—crocuses, snowdrops, bluebells, and primroses—that gave colour and life to the plain, ancient, weathered stone that was cracked in places and from which the villa had been built centuries ago.

"Oh, it looks lovely," Annabelle breathed as she stared up at the building. "Doesn't it, Mike?" Mike, still cross, grunted.

"I'll see you tomorrow then, Annabelle," Mary said as they got their luggage from the car.

"Yes, about eleven, I should imagine. I doubt I'll be rushing through my breakfast. I want to savour such a divine place." Annabelle beamed at Mary and gave her a hug. "Don't worry, we'll find Father Raphael, I promise. I'm sure it will all work out."

"Oh, I do hope so, Annabelle. I am so worried."

They said their goodbyes, and Mary turned to hurry back to the convent whilst Mike pulled the rope next to the wooden front door. They could hear a bell ringing a low note somewhere inside the auberge.

"Oh, isn't this delightful!" Annabelle squealed, her eyes wide and her mouth open as she looked from side to side. Clay pots with more colourful spring flowers were dotted around the entrance. She bent over to smell a bright pink hyacinth. "And it smells so wonderful!"

"It certainly looks promising," Mike admitted, finally finding cause to relax a little. "But no one is coming to the door."

"Look, there's a path that goes around to the back here. Let's follow it."

The path led down the side of the building, past a lawn of almost impossibly bright green grass. It was enclosed by shrubs and a stone wall that looked even older than the auberge. A wooden table stood on a patio partly in the shade of a lattice frame over and through which more wisteria vines formed a ceiling of lush, green leaves. It was past lunchtime now and the sky was the colour of Inspector Babineaux's 2CV, a bright clear blue. Mike yawned.

"C'mon, slowcoach," Annabelle called out to him, and as usual, her enthusiasm put a zing in his step. Mike picked up their bags and followed her.

Around the back, they found a door slightly ajar. Annabelle knocked. Not waiting this time, she pushed the door open and the pair went inside. They found themselves in a beautiful living room with oak-panelled walls and aged leather furniture. Shelves of books lined the walls. Directly in front of them was a narrow desk upon which the inn's guestbook lay. There was also a bell. Annabelle hit it smartly with the heel of her hand. "I've always wanted to do that!"

After a few moments, an elderly man with sun-browned skin and thick, grey-black hair shuffled through a door towards them. He was slight and stooped and wiped his hands on a towel as he walked. The door was completely surrounded by shelving. There were even shelves above the frame. Each one was crammed with books, many of them old.

"*Bonjour!*" the old man said, his voice a little hoarse.

"*Bonjour!*" Mike responded in such a bad accent that the man immediately switched to English.

"You are the English visitors."

Mike swung around to look at Annabelle and back to the old man. "I guess we are. I believe you are expecting us?"

CHAPTER NINETEEN

THE OLD MAN assessed the pair in front of him. Annabelle was wearing her civvies—a pair of jeans and a sweater on this occasion. Her clerical collar peeked over the crew neck of her light green pullover. Mike was less distinguishable in a button-down shirt, his collar undone and open, his favourite trench coat over his arm. "We only have single rooms. We are redecorating the suite now."

"Perfect!" Annabelle said. "That would be fine, thank you."

"*Bon*," the innkeeper said, "Follow me. *Je m'appelle Claude.*" He lifted two sets of keys from a board full of them and turned to lead the pair, very slowly, to their rooms. They travelled up a set of stairs and along a landing, stopping in front of an old oak door. The elderly man unlocked it and pushed it open. *"Révérend."*

"See you in a bit, Mike," Annabelle said as she wheeled her case through the doorway. "Meet you downstairs in ten minutes?"

"Right you are," Mike replied easily. He had realised

long ago that being around Annabelle required him to suspend his expectations and roll with whatever was presented. This was one of those times. He turned to follow the old man down the landing.

With a lot of banging and huffing, Annabelle wrestled her case through the door and stepped foot inside her room. "Ohhhhhhhhh..."

The room was magnificent. Early afternoon sunlight streamed in through the large arched windows lighting up the room, the ends of the beams falling on an enormous mahogany four-poster bed covered in cream silk bed linen. Vines of ivy were carved into the posts which rose up to support an intricately folded canopy of cream lace. Above waist-high, duck egg blue wooden wall panels, pink roses, and more vines decorated mustard yellow wallpaper. A matching chaise longue sat opposite the bed. To one side, a small table laden with fruit, madeleines, pain au chocolat, and orange juice beckoned.

Unable to resist and a little peckish after their long morning, Annabelle picked up a madeleine and nibbled it as she made her way over to test the bed. She slipped off her shoes as she walked across the dark stained wooden floor and bounced gently on the bed. It was as soft and light as the sponge in her little cake. She flopped back, feeling the silkiness of the quilt against her cheeks, the sunbeams that crossed her chest warming her. She closed her eyes and sighed. She couldn't think how life could get any better.

After he'd thrown water on his face and changed his shirt, Mike went downstairs. He browsed the bookshelves for a while and studied the old black and white photographs on the walls. They appeared to be scenes of the village from around a century ago. After a few minutes, he went outside and looked around the walled garden until he heard a noise behind him. "*Monsieur?*"

Mike turned to see Claude advancing. "May I offer you and your, er, lady friend some wine?"

"That would be delightful, thank you."

Shortly, the hunched innkeeper returned carrying a bottle of wine and two glasses on a tray. The tray shook as he walked, the glass tinkling. Without saying a word, he pointed at the wooden table on the patio. Mike dutifully sat, and the elderly man, with the ease of an action performed a thousand times, efficiently uncorked the wine and poured a small amount for Mike to taste.

"Good, no? It's made with grapes from a local vineyard. It has won awards. We are very proud of it here in Ville D'Eauloise."

"Delicious."

Claude filled Mike's glass, leaving the opened bottle on the table. He went back inside but momentarily returned with a basket of fresh bread, a dish of olive oil, and some blue-veined cheese.

Mike dipped some bread in the oil and chewed it lazily. He sipped some of his wine. He looked at his watch. There was no sign of Annabelle. He finished up his glass and poured himself another. He could get used to this.

CHAPTER TWENTY

"MIKE! MIKE! WAKE up!" Annabelle shook him gently. "You won't sleep tonight if you're not careful."

"What? Oh." Halfway down his third glass of wine, with his arms folded across his chest, Mike had fallen asleep in the sun. He was now sporting a pink nose.

"What's been going on here?" Annabelle looked a little sleepy herself, like she'd also just awoken from a nap. She had changed into a sundress and plonked a straw hat at an angle on her head.

"Claude made us lunch. I ended up eating and drinking most of it, sorry."

Annabelle laughed and picked up the bottle. It was still a third full.

"Mind if I do?" she said.

"You go ahead," Mike said, struggling to sit up. "I think I've had quite enough."

"Ah, just have a little. Keep me company." Annabelle sloshed a small amount into his glass and a significantly larger amount into her own before breaking off a chunk of the cheese and ripping off a piece of bread. "Mmmm," she murmured as she closed her eyes. "This is heavenly. Would you like some?" She offered some of the bread and cheese to Mike but he waved it away.

"It isn't really my cup of tea."

Annabelle shrugged. "You're missing out. Once you've tried a really good smelly cheese, you'll never go back. It is simply divine." Annabelle turned her face to the sun, savouring the taste of cheese on her tongue and the warmth on her cheeks. "Oh! You should see my room! There's a four-poster bed and a chaise longue."

"Not a single room then."

"Oh! No." Annabelle giggled. "My bath has feet and there are all these fabulous patterns in the floor tile. My, my, I feel like Marie Antoinette at the court of Louis XVI. Except of course, I wouldn't tell anyone to eat cake."

Mike laughed. "Marie Antoinette? You? Hardly. Joan of Arc, more like."

Annabelle was unable to reply, having just popped another mouthful of bread and cheese into her mouth. She chewed, gesticulating with her hands until she swallowed. "What about you? What's your room like?"

"Um, truth be told, I didn't notice. It has a bed, a bathroom. You know, the things you need." Mike had had other things on his mind. "I thought the owner said he had only single rooms."

"Hmm, I think he was protecting my virtue." Annabelle grinned and snorted at the same time. This culminated in a coughing fit. Mike patted her on the back.

It was late afternoon now, and they were bathed in a sunny warmth that was in stark contrast to the showers and cool temperatures they had experienced earlier in the day.

Annabelle held up her wine glass. "To a wonderful trip!" she said.

Mike clinked his glass against hers, and they sipped in unison. Annabelle savoured the ruby-coloured liquid.

"Rather good, isn't it?" Annabelle said.

Mike watched her lean her head back and breathe in the fragrant air around them. After a while, she looked at the inspector, her eyes soft, her mouth curved gently into a small smile.

"What?" Mike said, looking down at himself in case there was a stain on his shirt. "What is it?"

"We should really get you a decent coat," she said. "Something more suitable than the one you've got."

"What's wrong with the one I've got?" Mike said. He liked his trench coat. He'd had it for years.

"Oh, nothing," Annabelle said. "I just think you'd look rather dashing in something more stylish."

Mike grunted. "More like Inspector Bambino, you mean."

Annabelle chuckled. "*Babineaux*," she corrected. "He is rather elegant, isn't he?"

"Pfft. He looks ridiculous—you know he combs that moustache don't you?"

"You're just jealous," Annabelle chided, smiling as she sipped her wine.

"Of *him?*" Mike exclaimed. "A man who looks like he spends more time putting God-knows-what in his hair than he does doing police work?"

"God probably does know what he puts in his hair, actually. Shall I ask him?"

The inspector growled. "Don't worry," Annabelle said reassuringly after a pause. "I'm not about to run off with a French detective."

Mike broke into a smile, unable to be irritable any longer. "I doubt it would work anyway. Joan of Arc meets Inspector Clouseau—hardly a match made in heaven, is it? His magnifying glass versus your sword? It would be off before it even got started. His head, I mean. I may not know much, but I know when to let you have yours."

CHAPTER TWENTY-ONE

"OH, YOU ARE naughty, Mike!" Annabelle laughed.

Mike laughed with her before pouring her some more wine. "But if the post-mortem results come back positive and the priest didn't die of natural causes, I do think he might be right about the killer, however."

Annabelle frowned. "That Father Raphael did it?"

"Yes, unfortunately. I hope he's wrong, for Mary's sake, but the circumstances are pretty damning. He must have known all Father Julien's little habits, foibles, and customs. He's outside the priest's office as they prepared for the service, then he scarpers when he dies."

"Hmm," Annabelle said into her glass, "I know it doesn't look good, but I'm sure there's more to it than that. I mean, what motive could Father Raphael possibly have?"

"We need more information."

After a minute's thought, Annabelle stopped frowning and leant over the table, putting her hand over the inspector's to draw his attention away from the small bird that was feverishly investigating the wisteria.

"But," she began, "why would you commit a murder and make yourself the number one suspect by running away? Surely you wouldn't disappear from the crime scene as soon as it occurred. It would make you look incredibly guilty."

"Fleeing the scene of the crime is common."

"But not when you're poisoning someone," Annabelle said. "Poisoning implies forethought, calculation, subtlety. A mind that is careful, strategic, and deliberate. I can't imagine Father Raphael putting in all that effort only for his exit strategy to be to get away as fast as possible."

Mike thought about this. "Possibly. But then we have to consider something else. If Raphael isn't guilty, why would he disappear the moment Father Julien collapses? If Father Raphael were innocent, his reaction would be to go to Father Julien's side."

Annabelle hummed. "Perhaps he knows something but didn't actually commit the murder. Or perhaps he's attempting to take the blame for someone else? Perhaps he's been kidnapped. Perhaps he tried to stop the murder, and when he couldn't, he fled the scene, traumatised. Perhaps he's wandering about the countryside dazed and exhausted as we sit here drinking wine and eating smelly cheese." Annabelle's voice rose an octave as she ended her sentence. She half stood up in her seat, stricken at the thought of Father Raphael wandering the fields alone and confused.

"Calm down, Annabelle. We're straying into wild speculation territory now." Mike took Annabelle's hand and pulled her down into her seat. He sat rubbing her fingers whilst she settled herself. They sat in silence, enjoying the sound of the gentle breeze through the leaves of the trees and the birdsong that trickled in from the distant fields.

"There is one interesting thing about this," Mike said.

Annabelle raised her eyebrows in expectation.

Mike pointed to the bread. "This."

Annabelle smiled. "It certainly is interesting," she said, tossing another ball of the fluffy white bread into her mouth.

"No," Mike said, "I mean the fact that the convent makes bread. Seems a rather unusual thing to do. All that heavy fieldwork for a dozen or so nuns."

"Oh, it's fairly typical for orders to produce things. It's how many of them survived throughout history. Farming isn't so common, but they seem to make it work."

Mike nodded and leant back. "You should still talk to the nuns, though. See what they have to say. There might be some clues there. I could try talking to the locals."

"That's a good idea, but how will you communicate? I doubt they speak English, and well, I've heard your French."

"I'll point, wave my hands about like they do. Maybe I'll get Bambino to translate for me."

"*Mike.* Stop calling him that. You'll forget and say it in front of him."

A small smile crept across Mike's lips. "Yes, I might, mightn't I?"

CHAPTER TWENTY-TWO

ANNABELLE JUMPED UP. "Come on! Let's go for a walk. We should explore this place, get our sea legs."

Mike groaned. "Oh, alright." He pushed himself to stand, and followed Annabelle down the path and past the Mini to the lane beyond the walled garden. He looked up and down. Ville d'Eauloise was certainly a curious place. The ancient cobbled streets were so narrow that Annabelle had had to use all her Cornish driving skills to navigate them. Used to tiny, curving, undergrowth-lined lanes, she had handled the village streets with aplomb, but, unlike back home, she'd run the risk not of landing in a ditch, but of scraping all the blue paint off her car. Like the garden at the auberge, the lanes were walled on either side. Buildings loomed, casting shadows. It was late in the afternoon, and the shade made the lanes feel mysterious and not a little creepy. And they were quiet, oh so quiet. Where were all the people?

Hand in hand, Annabelle and Mike wandered leisurely down the lanes that meandered throughout the village. The hills were steep, and they had to be careful not to slip. A few of the homes had raised terraces. Nearly all were covered with pots full of flowers and always, always tables and chairs. Every so often, patches of raised lawn were held in place by the versatile, ubiquitous stone retaining walls that existed everywhere, creating verandahs, flowerbeds, and even stages throughout the village. A few of the lawns were scattered with bluebells. Along the way, they came upon a surprising array of animals. Chickens, goats, a couple of cows, and even a pig seemed to have free roam of the village.

"So they go in for containing their plants, but they don't seem so keen on the concept for animals," Mike said.

"Right, isn't it marvellous? Free-range in the truest sense of the word." Annabelle was charmed.

"One might think the two concepts were at odds with one another."

"How so?"

"The free-range animals eating the contained, immoveable flowers."

"Hmm, true."

A lone elderly woman in a floor-length dress and brightly coloured crocheted shawl passed them. She nodded. Annabelle and Mike nodded back. Annabelle attempted some French. *"Bonsoir, madame."* The woman mumbled indistinctly back.

"Where do you think she's going? It's only five p.m. and we haven't seen anyone except her," Annabelle said when the woman was out of earshot.

"I don't know. Perhaps they're all inside minding their own business."

"Doesn't seem quite right to me. I would expect them to

be outside on a lovely evening like this. Especially as it is still Easter."

"Perhaps they're in mourning for their priest."

"Maybe. Let's go to the square and see if anything is going on there."

When they got to the plaza, they found the church casting a shadow over it, making it cold and dark. It, too, was empty. No children were playing games, no one sat outside Café Sylvie drinking and chatting. There were no passersby.

"Huh, what shall we do now?"

"I'm a bit peckish. Fancy something to eat?" Mike said.

Annabelle thought back to the crumbly, heavy cheese she'd eaten earlier. "Oof, I'm not very hungry."

But Mike wouldn't be dissuaded. "Come on, try something. Some snails or frog's legs. Isn't that what we're here for? To try out the local delicacies. You can't go home and not tell Philippa you've had snails! Think of the look on her face when you tell her. Look, there's a restaurant just over there."

"Oh, alright. Just something small, though—and you have to help me."

The sign above the awning announced the name of the restaurant: Chez Selwyn.

"Funny name. And I thought France was all about outdoor dining," Mike wondered aloud. There was no one sitting at the tables outside the darkened frontage.

"It does seem strange. Perhaps it's closed?"

"*Ouvert*. That means open, doesn't it?" Mike pulled on the door handle. "Here we go."

The clamour that erupted from the open doorway evaporated immediately the pair went inside. Faces, open with curiosity, turned to them, eyeing the two British visitors with interest.

"Oh!" Annabelle breathed, a smile fluttering on her lips, unsure.

"Well, looks like we've found where all the people are," Mike whispered in her ear. He felt a bit hot under the collar, but he hadn't seen any threatening faces. No one seemed pitching for a fight. The place was packed.

"Bonsoir à tous," Annabelle tried. Silence greeted her words. No one moved. When Mike told Annabelle later that she'd bobbed a little curtsey, she had no memory of it.

There was a shout from the kitchen, then another, before a full-bloodied tirade commenced. Heads turned again as the kitchen door opened and a short, red-faced, round-bellied man in chef's whites stormed into the restaurant. He flicked a tea towel over his shoulder like he was swatting a fly.

"Watch-oo lookin' at?" the chef said to his patrons as he passed. He spoke in English. On catching sight of Annabelle and Mike, he stopped in his tracks. He lifted his chin and stared down his nose at them pugnaciously. It looked like it was the *chef* who was fixing for a fight.

"Yeah?" the man said.

CHAPTER TWENTY-THREE

"UM, WE WONDERED if you had a table. For two?" Annabelle said.

The man blinked and stared at them. You'd have thought he'd come across a talking donkey rather than a vicar asking for a table in a small restaurant in a tiny, out-of-the-way French village.

"English!" he exclaimed. He walked up to them. "So this is what you look like these days. I haven't ever seen one in this village. And I've been here since 1991."

Annabelle was flustered. The people in the crowd were murmuring to each other now. It seemed as though the entire village were there—elderly people, young people, children, and their parents. All ages were gathered at tables full of bottles and glasses and plates of food.

"Well, if you don't have room, we can j-just leave. It's n-no problem."

The man kept staring at her. His face was ruddy. Curls of his wiry, red hair peeked from beneath his tall white hat. His eyes were a sparkling blue and framed with white eyelashes and white eyebrows. Annabelle thought she detected traces of a Welsh accent.

"Leave? *Leave?* You're not going to leave." The chef took Annabelle's arm and gestured with a thick meaty hand covered in freckles and coarse white hair to a table for two by the window, the only one available. "I haven't spoken English outside of yelling abuse for thirty years. You, my dear, are going to sit right here and have whatever you want from the menu. On the house!"

"Oh, right, um, thanks. That's jolly good of you, but there's no n . . ."

"Thanks, mate," Mike interjected. "Very decent of you."

"Not at all, not at all." The chef clicked his fingers at a beautiful dark-haired woman hovering at the back of the restaurant. He wiggled his hand. The woman nodded in response and disappeared. The villagers seemed to have got over their shock and were now returning to their conversations, although judging by the glances cast their way, it looked as though they'd exchanged curiosity about Annabelle and Mike for talking about them.

"I'll send you my speciality for you to try."

"That would be lovely, Mr . . .?"

"Oh, what am I saying?" The man held out his hand. "Selwyn. Selwyn Jones. From the valleys of beautiful Wales originally."

"Pleased to meet you, Mr. Jones. You're a long way from home," Annabelle said.

"Ah well, it's a long story, but it involves a gorgeous French girl and a youth hostel. Swept me fair off my feet she did, but wouldn't leave her family, so I had to come to this forsaken place. She's long gone now, but this is my daughter Françoise."

The tall beauty to whom Selwyn had been signalling

earlier, floated over with a bottle of wine. Annabelle and Mike looked from the short, red-faced chef to the tall, graceful woman with big brown eyes and long dark eyelashes.

"Yeah, I know what you're thinking. How did an ugly mug like me end up with a daughter like her? Everyone does. She's a dead spit for my wife. But she's got her daddy's temper. There's fire in them veins, so watch out." The Welshman laughed, his smile making his otherwise threatening face far more congenial. "Are you looking into Father Julien's death?" the chef asked.

"Just helping out, you know, asking a few questions," Mike replied.

"Well, if you need any help, you just let me know." He lowered his voice to a whisper. "They're not too bright, this lot, and very close-knit. Suspicious of outsiders, you know how it is."

"We'll be sure to remember that, Mr. Jones," Annabelle said tactfully.

"And now, I'll get you your dinner."

"I hope it won't be frog's legs or snails," Mike hissed to Annabelle across the table when the chef had disappeared into the kitchen.

Selwyn reappeared carrying two plates. Mike's eyes lit up. "Sausage and chips! Now that's what I call a speciality."

"Ah, but not just any old sausages. *Andouillette de Troyes*, a traditional dish of our region. Enjoy!"

"Hmm, they're very good, Annabelle. Try one."

"Just a bite. I'm not very hungry."

"Well, give me yours then. I'm starving." Mike switched plates with Annabelle and tucked in.

"Did you like?" Françoise said as she came to clear their plates.

"It was delicious," Mike said enthusiastically, wiping his mouth on his napkin.

"Have you always lived here, Françoise?" Annabelle was curious that a lovely young woman would wish to live in such an out-of-the-way, isolated village.

"Yes, always. Like many of the people here, I can trace my ancestry as far back as the fifteenth century, and even though many of the younger generation leave for Paris and other cities, they almost always return. We have a saying, 'Wherever you go, Ville d'Eauloise will find you.'"

Suddenly, the sound of chairs being dragged across the floor started up, the big screen TV above the bar flickered into life, the noise of restaurant chatter died away to almost silence.

"Oh! What's happening?" Annabelle wondered.

"We're going to watch *The Life of Brian*," Françoise said.

Annabelle and Mike stared at her. "What? Monty Python?" Mike said.

"Yes, we do it every Easter. It's a tradition. My father introduced it when he moved here. It's his favourite film."

"Blimey," Annabelle said.

"We talk along with it too," Françoise continued. "Everyone knows the words. The children learn it at a young age."

"In English?"

"Yes," Françoise said, as though it were the most natural thing in the world for over two hundred French people to recite the dialog of a British comedy film in a language they didn't understand every Easter Monday.

"Well, this should be a treat," Mike said, and he wasn't referring to the crème brûlée Françoise had just laid in front of him.

"They really get into it, don't they?" Annabelle whispered a short while later. The villagers were entranced. All of them, from the oldest to the youngest, were focused on the screen, shouting out the dialogue in perfect time with the actors, clearly well-practiced. Groups of them were assigned roles into which they threw themselves with hand gestures, funny voices, and even props.

"Do you think they know what they're saying?" Mike asked Annabelle.

"Do you?"

"No, I think they are just having a rollicking good time." Mike was agog. He had never seen anything quite like it. "And it is very weird and strange. And I think we should get out of here before we get roped in."

Annabelle giggled. "Are you sure?"

"Quite sure. Come on, let's go."

And so quietly, with everyone absorbed and without anyone noticing except perhaps Françoise, Annabelle and Mike slipped away into the night.

"What do you think was in those sausages?" Annabelle asked Mike as they walked back to their auberge.

"Pork, I assume. They were very tasty."

"Hmm." Annabelle wasn't so sure. But she decided not to say anything. It had been a strange enough evening as it was.

CHAPTER TWENTY-FOUR

THAT NIGHT, ANNABELLE slept like a log—one packed with full-bodied red wine, some sausage, and a variety of French cheeses. Mike, however, barely slept at all. He paced around his room, performed sit-ups, showered three times, and as he sat on the edge of his bed, he turned over in his hands the tiny box he'd been carrying in his pocket.

"Annabelle, I'd like to ask you something," he said into the bathroom mirror, his voice low in case the walls were thin. He did *not* want to be overheard. "I know this might seem a little sudden, but I've given it a lot of thought and considered all the angles. It makes sense logically to me, however surprising it may seem to you. And I know there might be issues, but if you can think of no objections then— *Damnit!*" He banged his forehead with the heel of his hand. *"Too formal!"* He settled himself and tried again.

"Annabelle, I've had the time of my life since I met you. It's been really good. Really, really good. Would you—*No! It needs to be romantic!*" He shrugged his shoulders, and stretched his neck, first one side then the other. He bobbed on the balls of his feet like he was about to enter a boxing ring. "Deep breath. Come on, Mike, you can do it. Annabelle, your hair is as brown as burnt chestnuts, and your eyes remind me of the headlights on a perfectly-restored 1961 Jaguar E-type—*Oh bloody hell*—Why are proposals so hard? They make it look so simple on TV."

Mike had been through a proposal before, but last time was almost an accident. He'd been very young and a lot of alcohol had been involved. This time, proposing was an altogether different proposition. He had to get it right. Mike wracked his brain as he tried to recall his favourite films for inspiration. Very quickly, he realised there was a distinct lack of romance in John Wayne and Clint Eastwood films. Even his hero Humphrey Bogart failed him.

"Frankly, Annabelle, I just don't give a damn. Let's bloody well just get bloody married—bloody, bloody, bloody." He sighed once more before throwing himself on his bed and attempting to sleep again.

CHAPTER TWENTY-FIVE

MIKE AWOKE QUITE late, late enough to find Annabelle already sitting in the sunny courtyard with a cup of coffee and a plate of croissants in front of her. Groggy and grumpy, he squinted in the painfully bright morning sunshine.

"Morning," she smiled as he leant down to swap a quick kiss before sitting down, "did you sleep well?"

Mike groaned. "No. I think the sausages disagreed with me."

"Hmm." Annabelle had spent some time looking up what exactly was in *andouillettes de Troyes*. Somehow she didn't think Mike would appreciate what she'd learnt.

"Did you?" Mike asked. "Sleep well in that big four-poster bed of yours, I mean?"

"Beautifully," Annabelle said before winking at Claude, who was hovering in the doorway. "Could we have some more coffee, please? For my friend here." She turned to Mike, "Would you like to take it easy today? You do look rather tired."

Mike gave a wry smile, his grumpy mood dissipating in

the face of Annabelle's concern. "I would hate to miss out on anything," he said. "And we've got plenty to do."

Annabelle chuckled and pushed the remaining croissants towards him. "These are simply delicious, but I do believe I've had as many as I can manage. You finish them up. They'll make you feel better. After that, why don't we take those bikes for a spin?" She nodded at two bikes propped against the wall of the auberge. "It's a bit chilly this morning. It'll warm us up."

"Bikes? I haven't been on one in twenty years."

"Well then, it's about time you refreshed your memory. Come on, chop, chop."

Mike stuffed a croissant into his mouth. He grabbed another "for energy," before once more finding himself trailing Annabelle, who was already astride her bike enthusiastically checking out the gears.

"Let's ride to the plaza. It's all downhill," she cried.

Mike refrained from pointing out that it would be all *up*hill on the way back and cautiously tried out his bike with a couple of circuits of the path around the garden. "Okay, I think I've got it. After you," he said.

They sailed down the hill to the village centre, parked their bikes at the back of the church, and strolled arm in arm through the narrow, cobbled streets. Annabelle laughed and smiled like an excited child, pointing out interesting aspects of the architecture, even the grotesque gargoyles carved into the sides of the stone buildings, and delighting over the names of the shops. Mike did his best to match her mood and as he listened to her bright, cheerful voice, he kept wondering if perhaps now was the moment, but he kept deciding against it. Not when they still had a death to figure out. And not before he'd got his speech sorted.

After an hour spent exploring the shops in the village,

Annabelle, charmed by the exquisite handiwork of the village's craftsmen, bought herself an elegantly carved and painted figurine of a dog that looked rather like Magic. After that, she was satisfied enough to retreat to the auberge. They returned to their bikes. Strapped to the back of Mike's was a cage with two live chickens inside.

"What the . . ." Mike said. He looked around. Two young women were standing in the shadows, laughing. He pointed at the chickens. This only made the two women laugh even more before they scurried away.

"They mean for you to take them to your auberge, Inspector." It was Selwyn. He was polishing the tables outside his restaurant. "That's how we do things here."

Mike stared at the chickens. They looked at him without blinking. One let out a cluck. The other bobbed its head. "Are you sure?"

"Quite sure, boyo."

"What will happen to them then?"

Selwyn stared at him, then drew his finger across his neck. "Go on, it won't kill you."

Mike looked at Annabelle. She shrugged. He blew out his cheeks. "Okay, okay, if you can't beat 'em, join 'em, I suppose, but don't you tell anyone about this back home. Promise?"

Annabelle ducked her head. "Yes, sir!" she said gravely.

"Are you taking the mickey?"

"No, no, no." Annabelle looked over at Selwyn. He winked.

And so Mike got on his bike and wobbled off, sending the chickens into a bobbing and clucking frenzy that lasted all the way up the hill to the auberge.

Mary was waiting for them. "Annabelle, Inspector—I'm sorry I left you to yourselves. I had meant to come and meet you earlier this morning, but things have been chaotic at the convent and . . ."

"It's alright," Annabelle reached out to gently rub her friend's arm, her soothing voice calming Mary. "We went for a lovely bike ride, then we walked around the village. I got this dog figurine, and Mike got these . . . chickens."

Mary smiled meekly, her face strained with anxiety. "I see . . ." she began slowly. "Would you like to do something with them? Before you speak to the nuns, I mean. I can take you to the convent and introduce you. We were all there when Father Julien . . . when, you know." Mary's voice trailed off to a whisper.

Mike and Annabelle looked at each other. "We'd very much like to do that," the inspector said. "And take a look around the convent, if that's alright."

"I'm sorry." Mary held up her hand like a policeman directing traffic. "It's not." Her voice was sharp. Mike blinked in surprise. "No men are allowed at our convent. Mother Superior is adamant. Even our plumbers and repairpersons are female. They're called in from outside the village if necessary. We've even had women from the village learn trades usually performed by men because they know they can count on us as customers."

"Oh, that's quite alright," Annabelle said. She looked at Mike. "I can go along on my own. You could talk to the villagers like we discussed?" Mike looked at the chickens.

Before he could answer, Mary spoke again. "Inspector Babineaux would like to see you, Inspector. Apparently, he has some news." Mike suppressed a deep groan, squeezing his eyes tight to avoid expressing how he felt.

"Perfect!" Annabelle said. "You meet with Inspector Babineaux, and I'll speak to the nuns."

Mike opened his eyes. "Yes . . ." he said slowly. "Perfect." He took the cage containing the chickens from his bike and carried them inside to Claude.

CHAPTER TWENTY-SIX

SET AGAINST THE medieval charm of the sleepy village, St. Agnès convent fit right in. As Mary led her along the winding path towards it, Annabelle was impressed. Like the church in the centre of the village, the building stood large and proud, reflecting the importance placed on religion in the region. Also like the church, the convent was made of old blocks of stone, darkened and cracked with age and carpeted in places with moss.

There were wings on either side of the main building, like an "H" if viewed from above. Covered archways ran around the outside. A pair of heavy, arched black wooden doors were set into the building, and small, barred windows peeped out from the thick stones as though shrewdly keeping an eye on things. A path ran past flourishing vegetable and flower gardens and through a gap in a hedge to the open fields in the valley beyond.

Annabelle found herself gawping as she neared it, full of awe at the stark contrast of the solid, dark stone building against the light, vivid greens and yellows of the rolling hills behind it. The surrounding countryside was brightened by a morning sun that was slowly heating up the atmosphere. Annabelle could see the dew from the ground evaporating into the air forming a mysterious, romantic haze.

"That's remarkable," she said, almost to herself.

"What is?" Sister Mary replied. "Oh, yes, it's beautiful, isn't it? And so restful, contemplative. It's been good to be here. I have been able to . . . well, think."

Annabelle turned to look at her friend. "Are things alright, Mary? I mean, from even before this latest business. You seem a bit out of sorts."

"Oh, that's just because of what has happened. I'm fine, otherwise. Perfectly fine." Mary swung her arms before forcing them still. "It's quiet here. We are fortunate that we are off the beaten path. It would be terrible if we became a tourist hotspot. We occasionally get the odd artist dropping by—female, of course, but that's about it. The convent was formerly a monastery, and many say it was the second building constructed in the village after the church. The village arose around it to farm the land and serve the monks. But, well, it has quite a gruesome history . . ."

"Tell me."

"Not here exactly, but not far from here, sometime in the 5th century, a young woman named Agnès was killed quite brutally on the instruction of a Roman Emperor. She wouldn't stop performing miracles, or so the story goes. On her death, she became a martyr, and relics that are supposedly her remains are tucked away at the church. They are considered very valuable. Pilgrims drop by to see them sometimes."

"Interesting," Annabelle said, "if a bit morbid. What are those buildings over there?" She pointed to a huge stone barn alongside which ran a small river. An enormous wheel hung off the side of the building. A short distance away, surrounded by weeds and overgrowth, was a large, wooden shed.

"The one on the left is where we work."

"Making the bread?"

"Yes. There's a mill, a granary where we store our flour, and a bakery. We work shifts, taking turns to get up early. We are on a strict rota."

"Hmm."

"The other is just a shed where we keep all our bits and bobs."

"Like what?"

"Spare parts for our machinery, bikes, ropes, the normal things you keep in a shed, really. And over there are our wheat fields and orchards. Apple and fig trees. Oooh, we make the most wonderful jam. It's sold in some of the most expensive shops in Paris."

Mary waited for a response, but Annabelle was deep in thought. They walked across an old bridge that passed over the river. Annabelle gazed around. There was a feeling of peace and holiness about the convent and its grounds, something Annabelle knew well. It immediately made her think of Mother Superior's hard eyes. Protecting her territory seemed very important to the convent's most senior of nuns.

"Are you sure it's alright for me to just walk in like this?" she asked Mary.

"Oh yes, Mother Superior knows you're coming."

"And the other nuns?"

Mary sighed. "They're fine with it."

Annabelle stopped and placed a gentle hand on her old friend's shoulder to compel her to do the same. "What *is* the matter, Mary?"

Mary stopped, turned, and looked up at Annabelle. "It's nothing," she said.

"Come on, Mary. This is me you're talking to. Annabelle."

Mary pulled a face. "I'm fairly new here, just a few months. Some of the nuns have been here for decades."

"And?" Annabelle asked sympathetically.

"I'm just being silly."

"No, go on."

Mary breathed deeply. "I'm not really close with the other nuns. They're perfectly polite to me and friendly enough . . ."

"But you're not having wild parties every weekend?" Annabelle chuckled.

Mary looked sad. "Or even friendly chats. They really are wonderful . . . I just haven't found it easy. I don't have a single friend here except for Raphael. Oh, Annabelle, I miss you more than ever. I've never been lonely before. Up until now, when I've been troubled, I've always had God, but even he seems to have abandoned me."

Annabelle put her arm around Mary's shoulder and gave it a squeeze.

"But loneliness is a small thing," Mary said, smiling as if she had released some personal burden. "And this is a place of contemplation and devotion. It's not really important. My feelings will pass."

"Everything is important in the eyes of the Lord," Annabelle said softly.

Mary ducked her head under Annabelle's chin gratefully. They stood admiring the view of the countryside, the rolling hills, and a chateau that stood many miles away on the crest of a hill. After a minute, they turned to walk back to the convent.

CHAPTER TWENTY-SEVEN

"SO MUCH FOR a romantic getaway," Mike grumbled as he pounded the cobblestones on the way to Café Sylvie, the café to which Babineaux had summoned him. He'd decided to walk this time. The French inspector had turned a table at the café into his "office."

"Second day here, and I'm spending it with a pompous French twit who wears two-inch heels."

"'Allo!" called a distinctive voice from a table on the café terrace. "*Inspecteur!* Come! Come!"

Mike looked up and saw the lounging frame of Babineaux beckoning him over like Mike were a child to whom he was about to give a few euros. His beleaguered colleague, Sergeant Lestrange, sat beside him with his legs crossed and his hands clasped in his lap. His thumbs fidgeted with one another.

"Good day, Inspector," Mike said, shaking hands with Babineaux before offering his hand to Lestrange. The gangly officer had to hold back his cuff to take it. "Sergeant."

"'Allo," the younger man said. Mike realised now that

the confused expression on the sergeant's face was permanent.

"Sit! Sit!" urged Babineaux, patting the chair beside him. "Where iz *Révérend* Annabelle, may I ask?"

"She has gone to the convent. She's currently talking to the nuns."

"Aha!" Babineaux said, pointing his finger into the air. "Very good! Two amateur detectives separating to cover more ground! Clever!" He slapped Mike on the shoulder hard.

Mike closed his eyes. "I'm not an amateur, and I can assure y . . ."

"You are in an amateur *capacité, Inspecteur*."

Mike bristled. "What did you want to talk to me about?" he asked impatiently.

Babineaux delicately sipped from his coffee cup before placing it back on the saucer. He squinted mischievously and rubbed his palms together.

"It iz very interesting," he said, pronouncing his consonants in the slow, drawn-out way Mike already recognised as one of the French inspector's mannerisms. "First of all, we confirmed ze death was caused by ze poisoning. Ze signs were all zere. It was definitely murder."

"Okay, good. Progress. What's the interesting part?"

Babineaux smiled and leant in slightly, sliding a slim finger across his even slimmer moustache. "It was a gradual poisoning!"

Mike waited. There was more to come, he knew it, but he would not give Babineaux the satisfaction of asking what it was.

Babineaux leant forwards even further. Instinctively, Mike sat back. "Ze poison was not given in one killing dose,"

Babineaux continued, as if reading a horror story, "but in small pieces!"

"How is that possible?"

"I am told zat if tiny amounts of ze poison are given in zis manner *régulièrement*, ze probability of ze death increases until it iz *inévitable!*" Babineaux widened his eyes and exaggerated the last word like he was telling a story to a child. "But almost undetectable. Death comes from ze secondary problem like an 'eart attack, as in Father Julien's case."

"What kind of poison?"

"We don't know. Zey cannot find it. Zere is nothing in Father Julien's stomach except for ze rye bread and ze red wine and some over-ze-counter painkiller. Zeems 'e 'ad an 'eadache."

Mike leant back and folded his arms. He scanned the great plaza in front of the church before turning back to the French detective. "There's more, isn't there?" Mike asked.

"Oh yes!" Babineaux replied, jabbing his finger in the air. "Zat iz just ze beginning, my friend. Zis iz a very curious case indeed."

CHAPTER TWENTY-EIGHT

AFTER AN HOUR at the convent, Mary had shown Annabelle almost every part of it; the spartan rooms, the gardens, and the efficiently-run farming and milling operation. Annabelle found herself impressed, not just by the peaceful environment but by the organised daily routines by which the nuns lived. With Mary as translator, Annabelle spoke to the sisters as she came upon them, but she found, much as Mary had described, that the nuns, whilst polite and welcoming, were distant. The sisters spoke quietly, mostly to each other, and once they had offered a polite greeting and confirmed they had no information that would help the investigation into Father Julien's death, they quickly disappeared to carry out their duties.

"I wish I were so disciplined," Annabelle said to Mary. "How many of you are there?"

"Including Mother Superior, thirteen. A baker's dozen." Mary smiled at her little joke.

"We've talked to eight. You and Mother Renate make ten. Just three more left."

"Okay, we'll find them, but I need to hang laundry in the garden. Would you like to have a cup of tea whilst you wait for me?"

"No, I would like to help you with your laundry."

"Oh, there's no need, Annabelle."

"I insist. Look, we haven't talked to *that* nun." Annabelle pointed to a tall, young woman who was pegging out undergarments. "You never know what might come up. I bet many a secret has been shared across a line, a few pegs, and a row of freshly washed knickers."

"Alright, if you insist." Mary handed Annabelle a basket of laundry. Annabelle set about pegging cotton sheets to a washing line that zig-zagged its way between posts stuck into the ground next to the orchards where fig and apple trees spread out in rows as organised and structured as the nuns' daily lives. A set of posts over, the tall nun was shaking out a vest.

"Annabelle, this is Véronique. Véronique, this is Reverend Annabelle. She's from England. Véronique speaks English, Annabelle," Mary said.

"Pleased to meet you," the nun said, quickly pegging her vest to the line before offering her hand, her head hung low so that Annabelle couldn't quite tell if she was even looking at her. She took the young woman's thin, soft hand in hers.

"Véronique is relatively new here," Mary added.

"Hello Sister," Annabelle said to the young woman.

"Oh, I am not a sister. I am merely an aspirant."

"Ah," Annabelle said, swinging her eyes to look at Mary for an explanation.

"Véronique is trying us out for size, Annabelle. To see if this is the life for her and for us to see if she would fit in."

Slowly, Véronique raised her eyes to meet Annabelle's,

and the reverend found herself almost stunned by the young woman's beauty. All the nuns possessed the fairness of features that came from pure living, clean air, and fresh food, but Véronique was even more striking. Her cheeks were rosy, and a pale scar below her eyebrow stood out, but what made her attractiveness even more noticeable was the deeply sad expression she wore. Her big green eyes were luminous and moist, her full red lips parted slightly. As befit her status as a temporary member of the order's community, Véronique wore street clothes—a button-down shirt underneath black dungarees. "I have been looking around the convent and spending my time here working and praying. It's a wonderful, holy place and so very productive."

"It certainly appears a hive of industry," Annabelle replied. "You all seem very gainfully employed."

"We are doing God's work. Are you here to find out who killed Father Julien?" Véronique asked, her voice still soft, yet rising with hope.

"Not exactly," Annabelle said. "But I am doing my best to help." Véronique nodded and lowered her head again.

"Perhaps you can tell me what Father Julien was like?" Annabelle asked.

"Father Julien was a wonderful priest," Véronique began. "He was wise, loyal, and generous. He was private, but he always had time for those who needed him. He would mentor me about the life of a nun and help me explore if it was for me. I had several private audiences with him."

Véronique's features glowed, her eyes shining as she spoke of the priest. Annabelle caught a glimpse of her beautiful almond-shaped eyes brightening before they were weighed down by sorrow once more. The young woman looked down at the grass again and said, more softly, "He was a Godly man. It is unspeakably terrible what happened to him."

"And what about young Father Raphael? Did you know him at all?"

"Oh no, I didn't know him to speak to. Just by sight and to say 'hello,' that's all."

"How do you like it here? Do you think you will stay?"

Véronique looked from Annabelle to Mary and back again, a little alarmed. "I do like it here. Mother Renate is a wonderful Mother Superior, so kind and strong. But I have no decision to make. My prayers are very consistent. I am waiting for God to instruct me. As yet, I am still waiting."

"Véronique!" A cry came from a few yards away. Another nun, around the same age but shorter and plumper, came striding towards them. She said something in French fast that Annabelle didn't catch.

"Excuse me, Reverend. I have to go to the bakery. It was nice to have met you. *Au revoir*."

"*Au revoir*, Véronique," Annabelle replied, watching as the beautiful aspirant seemingly floated across the grass despite her dungarees.

CHAPTER TWENTY-NINE

PANTING, THE OTHER nun arrived to take over Véronique's task. A sheen of sweat was apparent on her forehead where it met the white coif to which her black veil was attached. She wore thick glasses that magnified her eyes to an improbable size.

"Annabelle, this is Sister Josephine." Mary proceeded in French to introduce Annabelle to the new nun.

"I know who she is, Mary," Sister Josephine snapped. She spoke perfect English. Mary stopped as though she had been slapped. She coloured before raising her palm to her cheek to cool it.

"Pleased to meet you, Sister," Annabelle said. She inhaled slowly to calm herself.

"I hear you're asking about Father Raphael."

"Amongst other things, yes."

"I have some information for you."

"Oh?"

The nun thrust her chin out. She flashed her eyes at Annabelle and nodded in Mary's direction.

"I shall continue this whilst you talk," Mary said. Her

lips pinched, she picked up her basket of damp laundry and moved off to the other end of the washing line.

Annabelle watched Mary walk away, dignity etched into her posture. The vicar turned her attention to the nun before her, whose breathing had eased now.

"That Father Raphael was not what he seemed," Sister Josephine hissed. "He wasn't always a priest, you know."

Annabelle smiled evenly. "Of course not. None of us were."

"But some come to it later than others, if you know what I mean."

"How so?" Annabelle kept her expression measured, determined not to feed this insensitive, over-excitable nun further.

Sister Josephine took a deep breath, glancing towards Sister Mary. "Father Raphael led an *interesting* life before he joined the priesthood. He grew up in Paris. He drank. Lived decadently, so I've heard." Sister Josephine hesitated before continuing. "He was a . . ." She looked around to check that no one could hear. "He was a *model*. On the catwalk. On the front of magazines. And you know the lives those kinds of people live." She folded her arms. "Then suddenly—he became a priest! That's strange, don't you think?"

"There are many paths upon which to find the Lord," Annabelle said. "His is not new."

"Father Raphael had a long way to go on his *path*," Sister Josephine replied.

Annabelle paused for a moment. "What do you mean?" she asked. She clenched the inside of her cheeks with her teeth and tilted her head back, waiting for the nun to enlighten her.

"He was still a junior priest, an apprentice to Father

Julien," Josephine explained, her French accent more prominent now as she spoke louder and with more confidence. She leant in and shielded her mouth with her hand. "Despite how it might seem, I do not wish to speak or think ill of anyone."

"Sister Josephine, if what you know might help find whoever killed Father Julien, then it is a greater ill to keep it to yourself."

The sparkle in Sister Josephine's eyes got brighter. She looked up at Annabelle, then again at Sister Mary, who was busy pegging more wet clothing to the line.

"They were close, you know."

"Who? Father Raphael and Sister Mary?"

"Yes."

"What's wrong with that?"

"Nothing," Josephine responded. "At least, not for those who haven't devoted themselves to God. But Father Raphael is a priest, and Sister Mary is a nun."

Annabelle scowled a little as she tried to wrangle some sense out of what she heard. "Let me get this straight. You think that Sister Mary and Father Raphael's relationship is untoward?"

"Correct."

"But what does that have to do with the murder of Father Julien?"

Sister Josephine sighed deeply. "I don't know. I only speak of what I have seen. And that things are not *what* they seem." She leant in again. "Secrets are afoot," she hissed before taking a step back and speaking more loudly. "My thoughts now are only with Father Julien, God have mercy upon his soul." She crossed herself before turning around to walk off towards the bakery.

"Wait!" Annabelle called. But Sister Josephine disappeared, and Annabelle's shoulders slumped as she sighed.

Mary walked up to her. "What did she have to say?"

"Not much, to be honest. Self-important nonsense."

"She doesn't like Father Raphael and hasn't been terribly nice to me since I got here," Mary said. "I don't know what I did wrong."

Annabelle looped her arm through Mary's. "Probably nothing. Some people are just like that. Inexplicable," she said. "Let's go and have that cup of tea and hope Mike is having more luck than us."

CHAPTER THIRTY

MIKE SAT AT the table in the café, a half-drunk cup of coffee in front of him. Next to it was the small bowl of snails Babineaux insisted he try. Mike had eaten one, it wasn't bad, but he had other, more pressing things on his mind than indulging this pompous nitwit. He had done everything he could to turn the conversation back to the investigation but Babineaux seemed determined to quiz him about British police work. It felt, to Mike, like a form of assault.

"Do ze English spoil ze crime scenes often . . . ? Are ze regular police as incompetent as ze shows on TV make zem seem . . . ? Would zey ever actually consult a person like Sherlock 'olmes . . . ? How do ze English treat crimes of passion . . . ?"

Once Mike's temper was wound as tightly as the threads in the French detective's smart suit, he held up a large palm to stop further questioning. He was pretty sure this, and the snails, were a set-up. "Enough," he commanded, in the low but authoritative voice he used with truculent prisoners. "I don't have time for this now. Perhaps when we've made some progress, eh?"

Babineaux raised his eyebrows. "Huh?"

"Let's get back to the cause of death. You said Father Julien was poisoned gradually rather than with one lethal dose but that there was more to it. What did you mean?"

Babineaux leant forwards and smiled conspiratorially. "Look at zis," he said, pulling a stack of envelopes from inside his navy blue, double-breasted jacket. He placed them on the table and slid them slowly to Mike as if he were conducting a card trick, one eyebrow raised.

"What are they?" Mike said, ignoring the envelopes. He figured the safer option was to keep his eyes on the French inspector. There was no telling what he would do or say next.

"Ze safe. We cracked it open . . ."

"It only required a key."

"Well, yes, but zis is what we found. I must admit, a clever decision on *Révérend* Annabelle's part."

"They should be in evidence bags. Fingerprints, man!"

Babineaux's face froze for a second, his mouth open, as the implications of what Mike was saying sunk in. "*Oui!*" he said, nodding as confidently as he could. "Well-observed, *Inspecteur*. Of course, I knew zat. Just a little test for you."

Slowly, holding only the edge, Mike picked up the topmost envelope from the pile Babineaux had placed in front of him. Using a fork, he levered out the sheet of paper that was inside.

"Unmarked," commented Babineaux. "Probably placed under ze door."

Mike scanned the letters that were pasted haphazardly onto the cheap paper.

"What do they say?" Mike said. Babineaux translated for him.

"WATCH YOUR BACK . . . WE KNOW WHAT YOU DID . . . YOU CAN'T RUN . . ."

"These are death threats!"

"*Mais oui!* From our murderer, no doubt!" Babineaux tilted his head and nodded nonchalantly, his hands steepled in front of him.

"Do you have any idea what they might be in connection with?"

"Absolutely none. But it adds to ze mystery, does it not?"

"It most certainly does. I wonder what he was hiding."

"He must have been receiving zem for quite some time." Babineaux nodded at the pile of envelopes. "Zere are at least zirty 'ere."

"Have you tested them for a poisonous substance?"

"Ah, *non*." Babineaux pursed his lips and squinted. He wagged his finger at Mike. "But zat is a very good *idée, Inspecteur*."

"It's detecting basics is what it is," Mike said. "And we need to talk to people to find out what was going on in the priest's life that might have caused these to be sent."

"We 'ave spoken to everyone. We did it as soon as ze priest was killed. Zey know nothing. We 'ave reached a dead end, *Inspecteur*."

"Someone must know something. As you say, they're not postmarked, so someone in the village must have sent them. Someone is lying. We need to delve deeper." Mike threw his head back to drain the last of his coffee. "And I need another drink."

Babineaux watched the inspector as he disappeared into the café before slapping Lestrange on the shoulder. "Put those letters in a bag and get them tested. *Non!* Not with your hands! Use a napkin!" he growled in French.

CHAPTER THIRTY-ONE

ONCE THEY HAD drunk their tea, Mary took Annabelle on a walk around the orchard. Along the way, they came upon nuns wrapping the trees in nets.

"What are they doing, Mary?"

"They are protecting the trees from pests," Mary explained. "We don't use any pesticides or chemicals here. This is an area of natural beauty and habitat for several protected species of wildlife, so we use environmentally-friendly methods to protect our crops."

"That looks difficult and labour-intensive."

"It is harder to protect everything, and we haven't always been successful. Apparently, the grain crop got contaminated with a fungus once, and it was all lost that year. But overall, it is the right, sustainable thing to do. We must protect all God's creatures. Come late summer, these trees will be brimming with fruit."

Annabelle nodded at the working nuns as she passed by. Everything seemed pleasant enough. The sisters were faithful, took pride in their work, and followed their routines. They enjoyed basic comforts and a focus on simplicity—and yet when she had spoken to them earlier, Annabelle felt a lingering sense of uneasiness long after their conversations finished.

"Mary, it feels a little strange here."

"Really? How do you mean?"

"Well, when we speak to the nuns, and I mention Mother Superior to them, I feel a change. It's difficult to put my finger on the source, but I feel it keenly nonetheless. They talk of Mother Superior with an undercurrent of awe."

"She's an impressive woman, Mother Superior."

"She certainly is. And formidable." Even in the short time she had spent in their company, Annabelle could see how much authority Mother Renate had over the women who were, due to their age and their lack of worldliness, highly impressionable.

"I think she's rather wonderful in her own way. She's not soft and cuddly like you, Annabelle, but she has a certain . . . something."

"She does that."

As the light of the day began to fade from bright midafternoon sunlight into what would become a more subdued, deliciously-rich burnt orange sunset, Annabelle realised that whilst she had spent a wonderful, eye-opening, spiritual time at the convent, she had made very little progress with respect to Father Julien's death.

"Mary, there's one more nun I'd like to speak to."

"Yes, Sister Simone. She's Mother Superior's second-in-command. She's in charge of farming and production. She'll be in the bakery, setting up for tonight."

"Show me."

Sister Simone's lined and wrinkled face appeared to pop out from her traditional wimple, the white cloth that wrapped around her head, the sides of her face, and her chin. She blinked owl-like from behind thick glasses and was clearly older than any nun Annabelle had met that day. Nonetheless, as Annabelle and Mary entered the building, they saw the elderly woman lift a bag of flour easily onto her shoulder. Annabelle found herself pleased to be looking at a soft-faced woman with intelligent light-brown eyes who seemed incapable of deception, dishonesty, and pettiness. Simone had the look of a person who had seen much throughout her lifetime, not all of it pleasant, but who was better prepared than most to accept it.

"It's very nice to meet you, Sister Simone," Annabelle said.

"Welcome, Reverend," the elderly nun said in English. "Please, come in."

Annabelle gazed around the big, well-equipped room. There were shelves full of flour, long tables down the middle of the room, a large thermostatically controlled proofing cabinet in the corner. At the end of the room, huge ovens still emanated a warmth that Annabelle could feel yards away, despite the nuns having finished bread baking hours earlier. Bench scrapers, lames, serrated bread knives, weighing scales, loaf pans, and cooling racks sat on a counter against the back wall.

"This looks complicated," Annabelle said.

"It's not, not really," Sister Simone replied. Her voice was soft and calm. "It's an entirely natural process that we simply encourage. We try to use the old ways where possible—these are linen proofing cloths we use for the baguettes—but as you can see, we aren't averse to modern technology." Sister Simone nodded towards the tall glass-fronted proofing cabinet.

Annabelle smiled. "That's a rather nice way of looking at it."

"It is the simplest way. We like simplicity here. Routines we repeat continually. It helps calm the mind and enables us to focus on our Lord and his work."

"Sister Simone is one of the wisest women I know," Sister Mary said, smiling.

"That's a polite way to say that I'm old," Simone replied, straight-faced. Sister Mary laughed, long-since used to the woman's dryness.

"We've been making bread for centuries, as long as the convent has been here." Sister Simone stroked the worn tabletop. There were cuts, knots, and even burns ingrained into its surface. "These tables where we knead our dough are even older than me, if you can believe it. The crop logbooks go back to the seventeenth century. Ville d'Eauloise is a place where you hold on to the past."

Sister Simone's soft, calm voice made her words sound like poetry and Annabelle nodded respectfully. She would love her sermons to take on such gravitas so effortlessly. Something brushed her legs. "Argh!" Annabelle looked down and saw a big grey cat sitting at her feet. Black fur wound around its eye like an eye patch. It was the biggest cat Annabelle had ever seen.

"That's Poupon. Eats as much as a horse, but we do love him. He keeps the mice down," Simone said.

"He's a big chap, isn't he?" Annabelle said, eyeing the cat carefully. He looked like a giant beast compared to Annabelle's Biscuit, who was, no doubt, currently fast asleep back in Upton St. Mary. "Is the village as sleepy as it looks? What about crime? Do you need much security?"

"No, we're a convent on the outskirts of a tiny village hidden beyond a forest in a valley with one road leading to it—burglary is not a problem except for the odd few apples stolen by the local teenagers a few times a year. Our biggest problem is stopping the thieving birds. At least, that is, until Father Julien's death and Father Raphael's disappearance."

Sister Simone broke into a small smile. "Even a so-called 'wise' woman like me can't know everything. But generally speaking, Ville d'Eauloise feels like the safest place on earth. It's why this sudden death is so shocking. We are not used to such things here."

CHAPTER THIRTY-TWO

THAT EVENING, ANNABELLE and Mike quickly got ready and went out again, strolling to the plaza to have dinner at Chez Selwyn. It was the only restaurant in town. It was much emptier than it had been the previous night, and everyone was behaving normally this time. For their parts, the villagers seemed to have grown accustomed to the sight of the tall, imposing man and his equally tall, cheerful lady friend, and paid them no mind.

As soon as Annabelle and Mike sat down, they began recounting to each other what they had learnt during the day. They were so involved in their stories they barely stopped long enough to place their orders. After Françoise, Selwyn's beautiful daughter, had taken their order, Annabelle and Mike continued to try and fit their individual pieces of the jigsaw together. They leant over the table, waving empty forks in their enthusiasm. They jabbed at invisible threats floating in the air and jousted with butter knives to make their points. Annabelle nearly stabbed

Françoise when she returned to the table to uncork their wine.

"So the death threats sent to Father Julien had something to do with his death?" Annabelle said.

"We don't know that. It's supposition only at this point, but I'd bet my coat on it."

"I wish you would bet your coat on something!" Annabelle joked. Mike groaned. What was wrong with his coat? Was it really that bad? "So we can assume that the person who sent the letters killed him then?" Annabelle added.

"Right. There were dozens of them. Father Julien must have been receiving them for weeks, months," Mike said.

"Golly."

"And what's more interesting were the messages in the letters. A lot of stuff about '*knowing what you did*' and '*time running out.*'"

"What do you think it means?"

Mike paused as he considered Annabelle's question. "Sounds like Father Julien had a dark secret—or at least, someone thought he did."

"Interesting . . . But it only raises more questions," said Annabelle. She sighed and propped her elbows on the table, resting her chin in her hands.

"Right."

"What about the poison? Anything on that?"

"They've confirmed he was poisoned, but they can't identify what it was. Only rye bread, a painkiller, and red wine in his stomach, so perhaps he didn't ingest it. He could have inhaled poisonous fumes or absorbed them through his skin. Crucially, it seems he was poisoned over a long period. Not a one-time dose but lots of micro-doses that built up over time and eventually caused his heart attack. They're testing the letters to see if that was the source, but who knows how long that will take? It's like time has barely moved on here from when dinosaurs roamed the world."

"And a lovely place it is, too."

"What did you learn at the convent?"

"Nothing."

"You must have learnt something."

"I learnt that Mary is lonely there, that the nuns are a bit strange and unforthcoming, that they revere Mother Superior, that they make a lot of bread, and that they have a huge, grey cat named Poupon that even Biscuit would take notice of. I learnt that one of the nuns has it in for Father Raphael, but it didn't seem to be much more than idle gossip. Oh, and the village has something of a macabre history. Seems there is a relic stored in the church."

"A what?"

"A relic. The remains of a girl who was killed for her 'witchiness' back in the 5th century and subsequently made a martyr. Agnès. St. Agnès."

"Lovely."

"A relic like that, true story or no, will be considered a precious artefact imbued with massive amounts of symbolism. We should check it out."

"I can't wait." Mike sighed and leant back, crumpling his napkin in frustration.

"What now?" Annabelle said. "We've run out of ideas, it seems."

"We need to find Father Raphael," Mike said determinedly.

"But how? He could be anywhere by now." Annabelle put her elbows on the table and rested her face in her hands.

"Mary is still very hung up on his disappearance. She's convinced something bad has happened to him."

Mike looked out onto the plaza. Highlighted by the moonlight, a few couples strolled across it. It seemed virtually everyone walked or cycled everywhere here. They had only seen a couple of vehicles in the two days since they arrived. "I don't think so. I think he's still here, in Ville d'Eauloisc."

"Why would you say that?" Annabelle cried, astounded at Mike's assertion. "How would he go unnoticed in such a small village? Everyone knows him. It would be virtually impossible to hide here."

"I don't know, just a feeling."

"Just a feeling? That's not like you."

"You just said that Sister Mary was hung up on him."

Annabelle lowered her eyes and started pleating her napkin. "Yes."

"What do you mean?"

Suddenly reluctant to talk about her friend, Annabelle spoke slowly and carefully. "I don't know for sure, but the way she . . . I might be wrong, but . . . I've known her for a long time . . . And I think she might be . . ." Annabelle cleared her throat. "In love with him."

"Really?" Mike said.

Annabelle looked at him and blinked. "Perhaps he feels the same."

"But . . . but she's . . ." Mike trailed off before starting up again. "And he's . . ."

Annabelle patted a fingertip against her lips and blinked again. "It happens. It did in *The Thorn Birds*."

"That was a work of fiction, Annabelle."

"It happens, Mike," Annabelle insisted, her voice harder now, her eyes defiant, her tone earnest.

Mike softened. He gave Annabelle a look of such tenderness, her cheeks went a deep shade of red. "Then he's here. And if I know anything, it's that a person will do whatever they need to, to stay close to the one they love."

CHAPTER THIRTY-THREE

THE VILLAGE OF Ville d'Eauloise was small, but it felt never-ending as Sister Mary ran through its cobbled streets. As she lifted her habit around her knees so as not to get it caught under her feet, tears streamed down her face. She scrubbed them with her sleeve. She battled against a strong wind, but nothing would stop her.

It was early by anyone's standards. Only the nuns were up, the sun having risen just a few minutes ago. No one was around to help Sister Mary when she stumbled. Tripping on a kerb as she tried to take a corner at breakneck speed, she tore her habit when she trod on it, the hard cobblestones grazing her knee badly. She needed no help to get to her feet again, however. She was powered by adrenaline, shock, and desperation as she continued on, pushing herself to run even faster towards her destination. Finally she reached it, yanking the gate open and running up the path to hammer on the door, sobbing loudly and uncontrollably as her small fists pounded on the wood.

Claude opened the door quickly, scowling. He was

wearing blue and white striped pyjamas and a matching nightcap, the end of which was topped by a fluffy bobble. He even carried a candle. He looked like Wee Willie Winkie, or perhaps, given the expression on his face, Ebenezer Scrooge. He was cross, a state that didn't change even when he saw the disheveled, tear-stained nun standing in the doorway.

"Why are you banging so loudly at this time of the morning?" he asked Mary in French. "It's not even six o'clock yet!"

Mary answered by pushing past him as if he were a feather. She began rushing about crying "Annabelle! Mike!" every few seconds until they emerged, groggy and yawning, to see what all the fuss was about.

"Sister Mary?" Mike said, incredulously. He rubbed his sleepy eyes and then opened them wide to check they were working correctly.

"What is it, Mary? What has happened?" Annabelle cried, more alert to her friend's anguish. "Oh! And you're hurt!"

Sister Mary came to a stop in front of them, bending over to put her hands on her thighs. She gasped for breath. It was the first time she had paused since rushing out of the convent.

"Mother . . . Renate . . ." she said between pants and sobs. "Mother . . . Superior . . ." A deep breath. "Dead!" A few more pants. "Hung . . . herself . . ."

It was as though saying the words out loud made the tragic event occur all over again. Sister Mary gathered some oxygen from somewhere and wailed dramatically before beginning to cry violently. Annabelle pulled Mary to her chest, looking back to see Mike's reaction. He stood dumbfounded. He was certainly awake now. Annabelle took her friend to her room, and after giving her a cup of sweet, strong coffee, they met Mike downstairs. Annabelle drove the three of them to the convent, she and Mike listening as Sister Mary told the astonished couple what had happened.

"All the sisters gather every morning at five a.m. to pray together," Mary said, her sobs soft and stuttering now. "And Mother Renate always led by example. She was the first in the prayer room, and I've never known her miss morning prayers except for one time when she got the flu. So when she didn't arrive this morning, we knew something was wrong.

"We assumed there had been some emergency that she needed to attend to so we went to look for her to see if we could help. Some of the sisters went to check the kitchen and common areas. Some went to the orchards. We knew she wasn't in the bakery as the nuns had just come from their shift. Sister Simone, Sister Josephine and me, we went to . . . went to . . ." Mary was sobbing too hard to continue. Mike shifted in his seat to pull his handkerchief from his pocket. He handed it to her. "Thank you," Mary said, comforted by the kindness. "We went to her room, and then we saw her . . . hanging there." Mike and Annabelle swapped frowns.

"I screamed," Mary continued. "And then, I don't know, I just ran—all the way to you. I didn't know what else to do . . ."

"It's alright," Annabelle said, glancing at her friend in the rear view mirror. "We'll find out what happened."

When they reached the convent a few minutes later, Babineaux's distinctive Citroen 2CV was already there. Annabelle quickly parked her Mini beside it.

Even under the gathering light of dawn, the dark atmosphere that cloaked the convent was palpable. It was as if the calm, order, and solemn devotion that Annabelle had witnessed the day before had been tossed out and replaced by a force of chaos and fury. A trio of nuns stood outside consoling each other, crying into their hands whilst attempting to pray. Empty flour sacks blew about in the swirling wind that whistled as it flew around the corners of the building and through the covered archways whilst lights inside the convent intermittently turned on and off.

Annabelle and Mike passed the nuns outside, acknowledging them with a nod. Sister Mary led the pair inside the building, the "women only" rule abandoned. They marched along a long, empty corridor that reverberated with disembodied sobs and wails that echoed off the medieval walls yet they saw no one.

"Stay here," Annabelle said to Mary, taking her friend's hand. They saw the figure of the experienced, calm, but pale Sister Simone coming towards them. "We can find our way to Mother Renate's room from here. There's no need for you to go through all that again."

Sister Mary looked up sheepishly for a moment before nodding with relief. She turned to Sister Simone, who wrapped an arm around the distraught nun's shoulders and led her away.

Annabelle took Mike past another cluster of crying nuns as they headed towards the door at the end of the corridor, voices beyond it growing audible as they got nearer. When they reached the door, Annabelle stopped and cast one more look at the inspector. Then she knocked and turned the handle.

CHAPTER THIRTY-FOUR

MOTHER RENATE LAY on the floor. She'd been covered with a sheet, a frayed scrap of twisted heavy rope visible at one end, the tips of her toes peeking out at the other. Inspector Babineaux stood to one side. He turned his face slowly to the newcomers. Even the French detective's typical theatricality was dulled by the spectre of a second sudden death. He was solemn. Behind him stood Sergeant Lestrange, his perpetually alarmed eyes darting around, his mouth open. His lips quivered as though he were talking to himself. Across the room was Doctor Giroux. He had his back turned to the room as he put his instruments into his doctor's bag.

They all nodded and mumbled brief greetings before gazing at the central figure like it were some foul museum exhibit or an inexplicable piece of art. Instinctively, Mike stood next to Babineaux—the events at hand causing him to dismiss his previous reservations about the French detective.

"What do you think?" Mike asked, without taking his eyes from the figure on the floor.

"What can I zink?" Babineaux replied with a Gallic shrug. "She 'anged herself from ze 'ook. It iz obvious."

Mike nodded and folded his arms. He looked over at the large iron hook above the fireplace around which a short piece of rope was still wound. "What's that used for? Normally, I mean."

"No *idée*. Probably for 'anging saucepans and zings in ze fifteenth century." As Mike had done, Babineaux folded his arms and the two men stared down at Mother Renate's sheet-draped body, united for once in investigative camaraderie.

"One never knows what goes on in another's mind," Mike said after a contemplative pause.

"*Oui,* she must 'ave been devastated by ze death of Father Julien and tells no-one. Then, she 'angs 'erself."

"Yup. Seems an open and shut case."

"Really? But how can that be? It is *impossible*! Do you hear? *Impossible*. She was Mother Superior! She wouldn't hang herself!" Annabelle exclaimed, barely managing to respect the solemnity of the situation and contain herself. She took a breath and continued more calmly. "Mother Renate lived a life of devotion, of prayer, of Godliness. Why would she commit a mortal sin? She simply wouldn't have been able to do it no matter how upset she was."

Mike gently placed a hand on Annabelle's shoulder. "That's not how this works, Annabelle," he said. "I see it all the time. People in authority, people with responsibilities, they lose their minds. Things get too much for them. They can't think straight. They lose all perspective and the ability to reason."

"Mother Renate was a competent, capable woman," Annabelle insisted, shrugging off his hand. She was seething.

"They're always the ones who don't show it," Mike replied. "The ones that others look up to. You yourself said the sisters are in awe of her. Those who do this are often the ones with nobody to turn to, no one to confide in when they really need it."

Annabelle huffed, unwilling to relinquish the point. "She had God to turn to," she said defiantly. "*I think she was murdered.*"

Mike, lacking an answer and suspecting Annabelle wasn't his number one fan right at that moment, turned to Babineaux. "Inspector, what would you say?"

"We are all sinners, *Révérend* Annabelle," Babineaux said apologetically. "Perhaps ze Mother Superior expected a special *pardon*."

Annabelle put her hands on her hips. She stared intensely at the covered body on the ground, her horror and revulsion overwhelmed by the frustration she felt at the two policemen's resistance to her theory.

"I understand your willingness to find an explanation, *Révérend*. It iz awful. It iz shocking. *Terrible!*" Babineaux said, his shoulders level with his ears. He stepped closer to Annabelle, his heeled shoes clicking on the hard floor. He looked at Mike, then back at Annabelle sadly. "And as a respected woman of ze church, you seeing another respected woman of ze church . . . Well, I cannot imagine ze effect zis must 'ave on you, *Révérend*." Babineaux put his hand gently on Annabelle's arm.

Mike felt something rise within him, that same feeling that ran through him when he saw how easily Babineaux spoke to Annabelle. But this time, it quickly passed. He didn't want to, but on this occasion he agreed with the French detective. And for once, Annabelle didn't seem charmed.

CHAPTER THIRTY-FIVE

ANNABELLE TURNED FROM Babineaux. She looked past the body to Doctor Giroux who had finished putting away his medical instruments and was now standing in the corner looking very much like he'd prefer to be far from this morbid room and its occupants, both the dead one and the ones very much alive.

"What do you think, Doctor Giroux? Do you think it's possible that this wasn't a suicide?" Annabelle asked, trying to keep the pleading tone out of her voice and failing only slightly.

Doctor Giroux snapped to attention at the sound of his name. When he saw the expectant look on Annabelle's face, he took his glasses off his nose, fumbling with them as he did so.

"Ah . . . it is difficult . . ." he mumbled. "I am not experienced with such things. I have called for a pathologist from Reims. They should arrive this afternoon."

"But in *your* opinion," Annabelle said, "as a doctor, did Mother Renate hang herself?"

Doctor Giroux began breathing heavily, rubbing his glasses on a handkerchief as he considered Annabelle's question. He glanced a few more times at the body on the floor. Eventually, he shrugged and said, "Yes."

Annabelle sighed. Her shoulders slumped.

"All the signs," Giroux continued, "are that she hung herself. There's no sign of a struggle. Not on the hands, not on the face. The discolouration of her cheeks—it is distinctly suffocation."

Babineaux and Mike looked at Annabelle, expecting her to be satisfied with this expert explanation, and ready to offer sympathy once she accepted the unanimous verdict of the others in the room. But Annabelle wasn't yet done. She wandered over to Mother Renate's desk. Papers were strewn over a blotter. There was a wooden desk tidy, a pen with its cap off, a pencil sharpened to a fine point, and a cup and saucer. The cup was overturned, pale yellow dregs of tea tipped into the saucer. They were long cold. Annabelle idly picked up the cup. She sniffed before putting it down again.

"And as a man, a human being?" she asked Giroux coolly, her composure intact now. "I mean, that's your professional opinion as a doctor, but personally, what do you think?"

Doctor Giroux breathed so heavily that the sound filled the room. His lips quivered. He seemed almost frightened by the question. He looked down at the glasses he held in his hand and lifted them to his face, winding the wire arms around his ears.

"I am very God-fearing," he said, looking at Annabelle directly now. "I never miss church. I confess twice a week. I have spoken with Mother Renate many times and . . . and . . . I cannot believe she killed herself." He paused but then quickly continued on. "But please! Please. Wait for the pathologist. I don't know! Really. I don't know. I am not an expert."

Sergeant Lestrange walked over to the doctor and said something in French that seemed to calm him. Babineaux turned to form a tight circle with Mike and Annabelle.

"*Révérend*," Babineaux said, keeping his voice low so that his words could be heard by only the three of them, "*Inspecteur*. We waste time on ze 'if' when we should examine ze 'why' ze good Mother Superior killed 'erself."

"Do you think Mother Renate's death could be linked to that of Father Julien?" Annabelle asked the two men.

"Perhaps," Mike said. "If they were close, his death might have pushed the Mother Superior over the edge."

"I don't zink so. From what I understand, ze Father and ze Mother were not very close. From what I have 'eard, zey seemed to keep much distance between zemselves." Babineaux stroked his moustache with an elaborate flourish, ending with his finger pointing up into the air.

"Perhaps there was something else then. Money worries? A secret illness? Guilt?" Mike added.

Annabelle frowned and opened her mouth to say something before closing it again.

"We're all speculating wildly," Mike said. "We need more information, more evidence. We need to learn about the histories of Mother Superior and Father Julien. Inspector Babineaux, may we read your file on Father Julien? And Mother Renate's too, as soon as you have it."

Babineaux opened his eyes wide. "Ze file?"

"Yes," Mike said, his expression growing incredulous as his suspicion grew. "The files. Surely you compile files on your victims? Their personal histories, places of residence, bank accounts, work details, health records, that sort of thing."

"Um . . ." Babineaux trailed off, rubbing his thumb and forefinger as if still interpreting the request. Slowly he turned to Sergeant Lestrange, who was still talking to Giroux. He said something in French that caused the sergeant to look over and shrug, his angular shoulders lifting his jacket a full three inches before slumping down. Babineaux's tone grew tense and curt. The sergeant snapped to attention and made a beeline for the door, suddenly displaying more speed and coordination than he had in the entire time Annabelle and Mike had been in the village. Once Lestrange had made it safely out of the room, Babineaux turned to smile at the inspector. He rubbed his hands together. "Ze files are on zeir way."

CHAPTER THIRTY-SIX

ANNABELLE AND MIKE bid a sympathetic farewell to Sister Mary who insisted on staying at the convent alongside the other nuns. They went back to the car. When they got inside, Annabelle simply sat, staring forwards.

"What's wrong?" Mike asked slowly, gazing at her resolute profile.

After a moment's pause, Annabelle sighed and looked down. "I'm sorry, Mike."

"*Sorry?* What for?" A stream of ice stole across Mike's heart.

Annabelle turned to look at him. There was remorse in her eyes. "I thought this would be such a lovely trip. Quiet, inspiring, *romantic* even. And instead, it's become more like a busman's holiday for you. If you drove a bus, it wouldn't be so bad. But your work is quite horrific."

Mike smiled easily. "Oh, it's no problem. It was my suggestion to come here."

"I know . . . " Annabelle sighed. "But it was for my

friend. And I'm starting to think I should have stopped you."

"Annabelle," Mike said, stroking a stray hair from her face. "There will be plenty of trips, plenty of quiet, romantic experiences in the future. I care about making you happy, and if that means we have to solve this case together, then that's what we'll do. Lord knows that that blustering baby baboon, Babineaux, isn't going to."

The words slipped out easily, without any of the usual awkwardness Mike felt when he spoke so earnestly. Annabelle smiled at him warmly, and they leant in for a soft, loving kiss. As they pulled away, Mike heard the small voice that persistently nagged him. *Now?* It was followed by another voice, just as persistent. *With a body just a few feet away? Don't be daft.*

"What should we do?" Annabelle asked, breathing out. She still found it strange, a relief, glorious, to have Mike by her side. She loved being a team. She'd been alone, besides God, of course, for so long that having someone trustworthy to lean on was a new, refreshing, uplifting experience. She didn't ever want it to end.

"Breakfast. Obviously," Mike replied.

"At the auberge?"

Mike frowned. "The church square," he said as Annabelle revved the Mini's engine. "I'd like to check out something that's been bothering me."

By the time Annabelle and Mike were settled in Café Sylvie directly opposite the imposing church steps, the midmorning sun was high and hot. Now that the shock of the morning's ghastliness had passed, a steely determination to answer the many questions swirled in their minds. As they picked at the last of their light brunch—perfectly-soft croissants, lightly scrambled eggs with smoked salmon and dried figs—and drank some strong coffee, they gazed silently across at the church. Both were lost in their thoughts.

"What do you expect to find in the files?" Annabelle asked, breaking the silence.

Mike breathed heavily through his nose and wiped crumbs from his hands.

"Clues to a secret, perhaps? Reasons as to why someone would send death threats to Father Julien? A hidden shame that caused Mother Renate to kill herself? A link. Something. Anything. In my business, when you've been doing it as long as I have, you get a nose for these things."

"Hmm."

Mike wiped his mouth briskly and tossed the napkin onto his plate. "But that birdbrain Babineaux!" he said, glaring across the square at a plant pot. The French inspector wasn't standing next to it, but given the stare Mike was aiming in that direction, Babineaux would have burst into flames if he had. "How could he not have compiled files? I would expect better from an amateur!"

Annabelle put a calming hand over his. "It makes sense. They were both high-ranking members of the church, and they take their faith very seriously here. No one would have suspected them of anything, certainly that they might have secrets. They probably still don't."

"The cleaner they look, the harder we scrub," Mike grumbled. "That's what my inspector used to tell me when I was a sergeant. I don't care if they were living saints. If you ask me, the church is full of people with secrets . . ." Mike stopped himself. "Oh, I'm sorry . . . I didn't mean . . . You know . . . I just . . ."

"It's alright," chuckled Annabelle. "I know what you mean." Mike grunted apologetically.

Annabelle squinted. "How do you see me, Mike?

"What do you mean?"

"Well, do you see the clothes, the ritual, the life of my calling? Or do you see me, Annabelle, the person, the woman?"

Mike looked at her, puzzled. He had no idea what she was talking about, but he had a sense that he was being tested. It was disconcerting. What was the right answer? He looked into his coffee cup as though he might find it there. He felt the small velvet box in his pocket poke him in the thigh. *Now?* "You're simply Annabelle to me," he replied. "My girlfriend with a funny job."

Annabelle blushed and looked away. Mike looked to see if he'd passed. He thought he had. Not failed anyway.

CHAPTER THIRTY-SEVEN

"WELL," ANNABELLE SAID, changing the subject, "what can we do now? Apart from wait for the pathologist's results and perhaps those files? You mentioned something you wanted to check."

"Oh, yes," Mike said, looking immediately at the church. A wizened old man was dragging a brush slowly across the top step. "I'll pay the bill, and we can go."

"Do you think the church will be open?" Annabelle wondered.

"Why not? St. Mary's always is."

"Yes, but St. Mary's hasn't been the site of a murder. I think they've kept this church locked up if no one in an official capacity is in attendance."

"Well, we're in our official capacities. Come on, let's find out."

Mike led Annabelle towards the giant entrance of the church. Ahead of them, the sight of the hunched figure of the old man performing his steady sweeping motions across the steps in front of the giant oak doors seemed like the tableau of an elaborate life-size cuckoo clock.

"Excuse me," the inspector said, gaining the old man's attention. "I'm Inspector Mike Nicholls, British police, and this is Reverend Annabelle Dixon."

The elderly man's round, dark eyes blinked at them. "*Oui, je te connais,*" the old man said, nodding slightly.

"Ah, right." Confused, Mike turned to Annabelle.

She whispered in his ear. "He knows who we are."

"Okay, yes. *Door? Open door?*" Mike said, pointing at the lock. He made turning motions with his hand.

The old man spoke a little more hurriedly in French before looking at the entrance, then mirrored the inspector's hand gestures.

"Yes!" Mike said. "*Oui!*" It sounded more like "wee."

The man spoke in French some more, clasping at the ring of keys hooked onto his belt.

"*Wee!*" Mike called out again, even more loudly, as if volume would make his effort to speak French sound more authentic.

Eventually, the old man pulled out a great iron key and unlocked the door. He pushed it open. The door gave a long, low whine as it swung on its huge hinges. Mike and Annabelle nodded gratefully as they passed.

"*Ten minutes!*" Mike shouted. He flashed all his fingers and pointed at his watch.

The old man nodded again, ushering the two inside with a flap of his hands as if already weary of the inspector's attempts at communication. Once inside, Annabelle chuckled.

"What?" Mike asked.

"Nothing," Annabelle said, still laughing as she turned

to take in the giant room. "So what is so important, it would cause you to put on such a display?"

Mike stepped forwards slowly, treading lightly on the balls of his feet so as not to make a sound. He held up a palm to request Annabelle's silence. As he slowly crept up the aisle, Annabelle followed him with the same soft footsteps. The inspector's expression grew even more strained as he neared the altar until eventually, he sighed with exasperation and shook his head.

"The first time we were here," he said, "I heard a noise. Sort of like a distant knocking." He ran up the steps and stood at the altar table, the flickering candles warming his cheeks.

"You think it came from inside the church?" Annabelle sat herself down in the front pew.

Mike looked up and pursed his lips. "I don't know. The acoustics in here make it difficult to tell."

"What do you think it was?"

Mike frowned as he continued to listen. "It sounded like plumbing, but I've lived in enough rundown places to know that banging pipes have a certain rhythm to them. This was sort of . . . random."

"How do you mean?"

Mike shrugged. He started to walk backwards to get a better view of the sanctuary and altar. He looked up into the high vaulted ceiling of the church. "I don't know . . . But we've been here a few days now, and I've listened for any other sound like it. There's been none." Annabelle strained to listen some more.

"Gah!" Mike exclaimed, balling his fists in frustration. "Another dead lead! Another stupid idea! I'm doing the very thing I hate to see in other detectives now—grasping at straws—whoa!" he shouted suddenly. He crashed down the steps.

"Mike!" shrieked Annabelle, running to his side. "Are you alright?"

Mike lay spread-eagled across the stone steps like a stricken sacrifice. He pointed a finger in the air. "There it is!" he cried. "There's the sound!"

Annabelle froze mid-motion as if his words had turned her to stone. She was bent over the inspector, her arms out to help him.

"Do you hear it?" he whispered forcefully.

Annabelle gritted her teeth and wrinkled her nose as she struggled to make out any noise. Apart from the sound of a distant passing truck, she heard nothing. Annabelle looked down at Mike's pleading face, suddenly aware of how the scene of a fallen man and a helping hand from above must look in such holy surroundings. After a few more seconds, she shook her head. "I'm sorry," she said softly. "I can't hear anything."

"There! There! That was it, I'm sure! Quieter than last time, but I heard it!" Mike looked up at Annabelle's blank face. "Oh, never mind!" Mike took Annabelle's hand and made to get up but instead pulled her down on top of him.

"Oh!" Annabelle cried as she tumbled. Mike grabbed her around the waist, and together they rolled down the steps, laughing as they landed at the bottom.

"Mike!"

"What? It's just a bit of fun."

"We're in a church."

"No one's here."

"God is. God's ev—"

A creak sounded from the back of the church, and the doors swung open. In crept the old man, his broom in his hand. He stared as he looked ahead and saw the couple lying in a heap at the bottom of the altar steps. Annabelle was splayed across Mike, her hair over her face.

Mike twisted his head to look at him and waved. "*Bonjour, Monsieur. Comment allez-vous?*"

Annabelle stifled a snigger as she pushed herself upright. She helped Mike to his feet and dusted herself down. Mike grinned and took her hand, squeezing it gently as he led her towards the open door, the old man staring at them the whole while.

The irony of the situation wasn't lost on the inspector, however. *Typical, I'm leading her the wrong way down the aisle!*

CHAPTER THIRTY-EIGHT

THE NEXT DAY, Mike was up early. Earlier than Annabelle, earlier even than Claude. He always got this way when he was at a vexing stage of a serious case. The officers at Truro police station joked he had some vampiric qualities that enabled him to go without sleep beyond which seemed humanly possible, but none of them really understood the agitation that prohibited him from a good night's rest when he felt he had work to do.

After pacing up and down his room, flicking through a book he'd hastily thrown into his bag before he left home, and checking the clock every thirty seconds in the hope that time had progressed to a more acceptable hour, Mike finally got dressed and silently left his room. He moved carefully through the hotel and out to the table in the courtyard. The early morning hours were pleasing to him. It was still dark. Stars twinkled brightly in a velvety-black sky. No one was about. The auberge looked even more appealing under the shimmering half-moon.

The temperature was much warmer than in England. Warm enough that he needed no jacket to sit outside, yet the air was crisp and fresh. It was filled with the fragrance of flowers around him. He inhaled deeply, savouring the aromas of refreshing mint, pungent hyacinths, budding wisteria, and found a touch of cherry blossom layered on top. *No wonder the French have such a nose for wine.*

But the peacefulness of Mike's surroundings couldn't calm his racing thoughts. The case was troubling enough. It had been four days since Father Julien's murder, and they had few leads, no idea where Father Raphael was, and now another death. His hopes of solving the case quickly and enjoying the rest of the week alone with Annabelle, building up to his pitch-perfect proposal and an unqualified acceptance, were fading.

He pulled the small ring box from his pocket, flipped it open, and set it on the picnic table. He gazed at it lazily, the gentle moonlight amplifying the diamond's perfectly-cut dimensions. When it had come to selecting the ring, money had been no object. The inspector lived well within his means, and saved a lot. He had plenty to spend on an engagement ring for his beloved. The tricky part had been choosing the right diamond. And keeping it a secret.

There was a jeweller in Upton St. Mary who was highly regarded but had Mike gone there, he might as well have announced his intentions in the parish newsletter. Instead, following weeks of consideration, after visiting every single jeweller in Truro, and with the patient help of a kindly shop assistant who had, she told him, overseen thousands of similar purchases in her thirty years of service, he had picked out a brilliantly cut, sizeable but not ostentatious, solitaire diamond ring. As he regarded it in the early morning darkness, he thought it beautiful. If the response to a proposal were based on the ring alone, acceptance would be guaranteed. But there's only so much diamonds can do. And Annabelle would not be swayed by a mere bauble.

For the first time in his life, the inspector was genuinely afraid. He had faced down entire gangs of criminals by himself. He had taken blows during arrests. He had risked his entire career on hunches, and even gone toe-to-toe with a fellow detective during a corruption scandal that almost tore the station apart. But all of that paled in comparison to the challenge he faced now.

What if she says no? Mike forced himself to think about this for a moment. *She'd probably let me down gently, be kind about it, tell me to wait a year.*

Gazing into the sparkling diamond's multi-faceted surface as if it might reveal the future, Mike turned his thoughts inside out, knotted them up, and threw them over his shoulder before retrieving them and starting the process all over again until the diamond began glinting even brighter in the light of dawn.

Through a window, Claude caught sight of Mike sitting forlornly in the garden. Shortly afterwards, the aroma of brewing coffee mixed with warm brioche filled the auberge. Annabelle emerged, Pavlovian-like, her nose wrinkled in anticipation and an expectant smile on her face, unaware of her beloved's anxiety.

"Morning, Mike," she said, leaning over to kiss him before sitting at the table.

"Morning, Annabelle." He quickly pocketed the ring.

"We're like an old married couple, aren't we? Sitting down to breakfast like this every day."

"Not really, we emerge from different rooms."

"Apart from that."

Mike wasn't sure how to take this exchange, so he decided to concentrate on his food. Halfway through their breakfast of cheese, brioche, soufflé, and coffee, Claude reappeared at their table.

"*Inspecteur? Révérend?* Inspector Babineaux has just called. He says you are to meet him at his office. He says the files have arrived!"

"About time too," Mike said.

Annabelle looked at him like she would a naughty child. Mike quickly finished swallowing a mouthful of soufflé. "Thank you for passing on the message, Claude. Much obliged."

"Detective Babineaux has an office here?" Annabelle asked when Claude had left.

"Oh yes," Mike said drily. "It serves snails."

CHAPTER THIRTY-NINE

AS THEY DROVE through the streets of Ville d'Eauloise towards the café, Annabelle and Mike noticed that the villagers seemed unusually low-key. There was a sense of sadness that seemed at odds with the gloriously warm sun set in the clear blue sky. Father Julien's death had been public and dramatic, causing shock and grief. But as news of the Mother Superior's apparent suicide spread, the locals had become even more withdrawn.

Father Julien had walked the streets, given sermons to the villagers, and had known many of them well. He had his foibles, such as his penchant for pastries at all times of the day and how he would palm his hair with the care of a man about to hit the town. But he'd also been present in the lives of the villagers at their most intimate points—not just their births, deaths, and marriages, but via the confessional, their scandals, their money woes, and their darkest thoughts.

By contrast, Mother Renate had been a stern, imposing personality, more akin to a force of nature than a mortal woman. When she walked through the streets, it had always been with a destination in mind. Passers-by would not call to her but simply nod respectfully, expecting no more than a flicker of an eye in return. Children stopped their mischievous games in her presence. Adults refrained from small talk, jokes, and village gossip when she was near. Under her guidance, the dozen or so nuns at the convent led lives of selflessness, simplicity, and industry. And despite praying for many hours a day, they still managed to farm their land and bake enough bread to supply the village and those nearby.

As they arrived at the plaza, Annabelle and Mike bumped into Selwyn, the Welsh chef.

"Morning, Selwyn," Mike said.

"Mornin' boyo."

"Everyone seems very subdued," Annabelle said.

"Aye, they are troubled by the deaths, for sure," Selwyn responded. "This latest one has fair taken the wind out of their sails. To their minds, Mother Superior was too firm and forthright to die. To hear that she has passed is strange. To hear that it was by her own hand is unbelievable."

Annabelle and Mike went to the cafe and greeted Babineaux and Lestrange warmly. Well, Annabelle did. Mike simply nodded. Babineaux went one step further and used his old-world charm on Annabelle once again. He kissed the back of her hand. Mike suppressed an eye-roll, but he wasn't about to be outmanoeuvred twice in a matter of seconds and quickly won the race to pull out Annabelle's chair before Babineaux could do it for her.

After exchanging polite small talk about the weather, Babineaux reached into the tasteful, aged-leather satchel at his side and pulled out three folders.

"We 'ave the pathology report for Mother Renate. It confirms she suffocated. 'er death is consistent with 'anging." Annabelle frowned at this news. "And 'ere we 'ave ze victim's files," Babineaux said. He placed the files on the table and pushed them towards Annabelle and Mike. "I 'ave 'ad zem translated for you."

"These are the case files on Father Julien and Mother Renate?" Mike said, picking up one folder as Annabelle took the other.

Babineaux shrugged. "*Oui*. Please, read. We shall wait." He crossed his long legs and sat back.

Mike opened his folder to begin, glancing over at Annabelle who was already halfway down the first page of her papers.

They passed the next few minutes in silence, broken only by the occasional sip of coffee, the rustling of a flipped page, and the exchange of folders. Babineaux sat patiently, quietly exulting in his ability to produce something he was sure would impress the English people. Eventually, Annabelle and Mike set the folders down, and all three of them exchanged glances. The contents of the folders had given them food for thought.

Annabelle broke the silence. "So Father Julien was born to a working-class family in Nice in Southern France. There wasn't much on his early adulthood, but we know he held odd jobs as a labourer which must mean he was a strong, healthy young man. He entered the priesthood at twenty-eight, studying in a seminary on the outskirts of Nice, and then performed missionary work in Asia before returning to France and being appointed to the parish of Ville d'Eauloise."

Mike continued. "Right, and like Father Julien, Mother Renate was also born in Nice, but to a wealthy family. Her father was a major Catholic benefactor, donating huge sums after parts of the Nice cathedral were destroyed in a fire.

After she finished school, Renate left Nice to study chemistry at the university in Reims. Soon into her studies, she abruptly left and travelled to Switzerland, where she became a nun. As Mother Renate, she spent two decades travelling the world doing humanitarian work before eventually being assigned the role of Mother Superior at St. Agnès convent a few years ago."

There followed several moments of thoughtful coffee-sipping before either Annabelle or Mike spoke again.

"They were from the same city," Annabelle mumbled.

"And they ended up in the same village," Mike added.

"A coincidence?"

"Don't believe in them," said Mike.

CHAPTER FORTY

MIKE OPENED HIS folder again to check the dates. "Look here, they grew up in the same place. Then, twenty-something years after they leave, after all sorts of adventures, they both end up as Catholic clergy in the same, out-of-the-way, medieval French village miles from where they grew up. And they end up dead within a couple of days of one another. What are the chances of that?"

"So . . ." Annabelle began. She drew her words out slowly as she continued to think. "You think there's some connection between them, something related to their earlier lives that's behind their deaths? Perhaps they knew each other? When they were younger, I mean."

"Hmm, maybe. And why would Renate go all the way to Switzerland to become a nun?" Mike asked. "Why not train, or whatever it is you do to become a nun, right here? There are plenty of convents in France, aren't there?"

Babineaux nodded. "Indeed, zey are all over."

Annabelle shrugged. "There could be lots of reasons for it—space, fit, location. It's a decision that encompasses an aspirant's entire existence. And it's expected to last a lifetime! Perhaps she wanted to see a little more of the world and this particular order in Switzerland could provide that."

"But then why end up in Ville d'Eauloise?" Mike asked, butchering the village's name with his impatience and poor French accent. He didn't need to say the words "sleepy backwater," but they were there in his tone.

"A recommendation, maybe," Annabelle said. "If they did know one another previously, Julien might have known the convent was looking for a Mother Superior and suggested Renate for the position."

"Is that how they do it? They apply for promotions and transfers like anyone else?"

"Of course. And just like secular organisations, they often promote from within. But if that isn't possible, they will look to another."

"Hmph, not that much different from the force." Mike slapped his file down on the table and folded his arms.

"*Pardonnez-moi, Révérend.* But you are saying zat zis information is completely irrelevant?" Babineaux said.

"No, but it raises more questions than it answers," Annabelle replied. She gestured at the folder. "This all seems quite normal to me. Nothing extraordinary. Coincidences and similarities, but that's all. We are using supposition to connect the dots. We need more."

"Look," Mike said adamantly. He placed his palm flat on the folder in front of him. "There's a connection here. Two people who died under strange circumstances in this village grew up only a few miles apart before travelling the world and being drawn to the same place years later. I've got a hunch there's something in this."

Babineaux raised one of his fine eyebrows so high that

Mike wondered if it were caught on a fishing line. "Ze mind goes to ze romance, does it not?"

"Romance?" Annabelle said incredulously.

"*Mais oui*. Father Julien was young once, as was Mother Renate. Zey were ze right ages for ze love to 'ave blossomed. 'e was an 'andsome young man with muscles from ze 'ard work 'e did, and ze 'air 'e kept to ze end. Ze Mother Superior was most likely a girl of intelligence and wit before she added discipline and righteousness to 'er character. She 'ad fine bones, she could 'ave been a beauty when she was younger. These qualities are magnetic, zey draw zem to each other. Somezing rare amongst zeir peers, somezing only zey can understand. Zey walk along ze Côte d'Azur, talking to each other of ze divine beauty and poetry in ze Bible, sharing zeir thoughts zey never told anyone else, until it is impossible to imagine being with anyone else." Babineaux squinted and looked at his rapt audience, his eyes shining. "Zey discover zat they both feel a deep, devout love for not just ze Lord, but for each other. But 'er family doesn't approve. A working boy and a wealthy girl. Zey are separated, and she is sent away, but not before zeir passion overcomes zem and . . ."

"Okay, okay!" Mike exclaimed. "We get the idea." He glared at Babineaux.

Mike turned to Annabelle, waiting for her response, but she seemed lost in the scene that Babineaux had painted. She had a small smile on her face and a distant look in her eyes. "It's possible," Annabelle said dreamily.

"It would explain much," Babineaux said, adding a smoky mystery to his voice.

"Like what?" Mike demanded.

"Like why she killed 'erself," Babineaux said.

"I don't follow."

Babineaux grinned knowingly and leant back in his chair, shaking his head slightly. "Ze love of 'er life was murdered. Ze man she came 'ere to be close to."

"Hold on!" Mike said, waving his palms. "You're telling fairytales now. There's no room for that in police business. There's no evidence." He rocked back on two legs of his chair, his lips pursed.

Babineaux continued to look amused at this uptight Englishman. "All romance iz a fairytale in a sense," he said.

"Even *if* they were a couple *once*," Mike said firmly, "there can't have been anything between them now. It's ridiculous! I mean, we're talking about *a nun* and *a priest* here!"

"You are not well-acquainted with ze facts of ze romance, are you *Inspecteur*?" Babineaux's wry grin taunted Mike.

"What on earth does that have to do with anything?" Mike slammed the front legs of his chair on the ground and banged his hand on the table loud enough to turn heads.

"Calm down, both of you!" Annabelle said. "You're police detectives—not children!"

Mike hung his head. Babineaux offered a nod of apology.

"We don't know much," Annabelle continued, "so anything is possible. Yes, they might have been romantically linked at some point—however, I have to agree with Mike, it doesn't seem likely to me. We do have some kind of connection to work with, though." Annabelle sighed and pushed her chair away from the table.

"Where are we going?" Mike said, beginning to rise. Annabelle pressed a hand on his shoulder and pushed him back down.

"*I'm* going to meet Mary. *Alone.*"

"Oh, well . . . what about me?" Mike asked, suddenly feeling like a ditched pet.

"*You* should get back to finding Father Raphael," Annabelle said. "I believe he's still the key to all of this, and he's still very much missing." She looked at Babineaux. "He's *your* main suspect," she said, before turning to Mike again, "and he's the reason *you're* here in the first place. So I suggest you two stop your bickering and use whatever on earth they teach you in detective school to find him!"

Without a word more, Annabelle walked briskly across the plaza to her car. Slamming her door hard, she drove off, the detectives she left behind watching with awe and admiration.

CHAPTER FORTY-ONE

ONCE ANNABELLE DISAPPEARED from sight, Mike noticed with some alarm that Babineaux was eyeing him keenly.

"What?" Mike asked quickly.

Babineaux chuckled lightly to himself. "You are besotted, are you not, *Inspecteur?*"

Mike cleared his throat awkwardly and sat upright. "I don't see what that's got to do with . . ."

Babineaux chuckled again. "In France, we often talk of ze love. We feel it strongly, and we like to share our love with ze world."

"Well, I don't feel like sharing anything, thank you very much."

Babineaux performed his signature move. He leant back in his chair and crossed one long languid leg over the other, bringing his coffee cup to his mouth in a smooth, delicate movement. He kept the glint in his eye focused upon Mike, however, even as he set his coffee cup down.

"'ave you decided 'ow you will do it?"

Mike frowned. "Do what?"

"Propose, of course."

Mike's frown fell away, along with his jaw. He looked around furtively, checking that no one was listening before leaning forwards across the table. "How did you know that?" he hissed in a low whisper.

Babineaux shrugged. "I am not as incompetent as you zink, *Inspecteur*. Ze British always assume others are not as observant as zey are."

"Okay, but *how?*" insisted Mike. "Did you go through my things and find the ring? Do you have spies listening to me at night? Did Claude say something to you?"

Babineaux laughed and looked across at Lestrange, but his sergeant was busy solving a crossword. The older detective turned back to Mike and brushed his moustache, revelling in the other inspector's confusion.

"*Mon Dieu!* You are so typical of ze English detectives! Always looking for ze misplaced scalpel or ze stained 'andkerchief. It is a wonder zat two British people ever fall in love with such logic at zeir core! I suppose zat is what makes your fictional detectives so interesting to read. A French Sherlock 'olmes would simply look into people's eyes and see all zat 'e needs."

"Are you going to answer my question?" asked Mike impatiently.

Babineaux brushed his moustache again as if considering the request. He tilted his head. "You are agitated. Agitated, despite 'aving a wonderful woman by your side. A woman who is kind, compassionate, and devoted to you. You are in a picturesque village amongst beautiful countrysides with much to share with such a woman, and yet you act as if zere is some immense chore you must carry out. I do not believe ze murder is ze cause of your frustration—you are too experienced for zat. So what is zis *task* zat bothers you so?" Mike breathed heavily through his nose, but he could think of no response.

"For a man like you, marriage iz not a choice—it iz an *inevitability*. You are not reckless or overwhelmed by your passion. You are cautious and careful. You are British through your very core. Like, what is it you say? Ah yes, like a *stick of rock*. And especially when your lover iz a priest, zer iz little room for ze *living in sin* as it is called in your language, but is called *love* in mine. Yes, *Inspecteur* Nicholls, marriage was on your mind from ze very first time you kissed *Révérend* Annabelle, of zat I am certain."

Mike huffed and folded his arms. "I could sit back and make a few observations about you too, you know," he said grudgingly.

"But zer iz a *problème!*" Babineaux said, plowing on. "You speak directly, and plainly. Everyzing from your language, to your clothes, to your choice in *café*," Babineaux pointed to the black, unsweetened coffee that sat in front of the inspector, "indicates zat you 'ave little time for ze details, ze small pleasures, ze frivolous, zings zat are not, 'ow do you say, *pratique*. And to propose is ze opposite. It iz ze ultimate romantic gesture."

Mike sat quietly. He grew hot as he listened to Babineaux. He was conflicted. He wished he could conjure up a withering put-down, but at the same time, he felt relieved that the problem that had plagued him for so long was now shared with someone. Even if that someone was a tall, poncy Frenchman who looked like he wore mascara.

"Well, either way," Mike said finally, "don't tell anyone about this, okay?"

"*Bien sûr!*" Babineaux said, opening his arms wide. "I intend to 'elp you cultivate ze fruits of love, *Inspecteur*, not destroy zem!"

"*Help?* Oh, hell no. What are you talking about?"

Babineaux chuckled and kept Mike waiting as he sipped from his cup before answering. "I am offering my assistance to make your proposal ze perfect one."

"I don't want your assistance."

Babineaux laughed again. "I am certain you don't *want* my 'elp, *Inspecteur,* but I am also certain zat you *need* it!"

Mike looked down. For a moment, he considered the idea. Annabelle certainly seemed taken with Babineaux. She was often charmed by the Frenchman's way with words and manners. He tapped his thumb against his knee. But no, the idea was preposterous, ridiculous—a grown man, a respected police detective, taking advice from a lithe, lofty lothario who probably wore moisturiser? His pride would never allow it.

"No," Mike said flatly.

"*Non?*"

"No," Mike said, once again. "It's a silly idea. I'm not a teenager who needs tips on how to conduct himself. The notion is ludicrous."

With a customary tilt of his head, Babineaux shrugged and returned his gaze to the comings and goings of those on the plaza. "It iz wise to know when you don't know zings," he said softly, offering his words to the air and letting them fall where they may, like someone blowing on a dandelion clock.

Mike frowned. He wanted to get up and leave but found himself unable to do so. The men sat in silence, Mike still banging the side of his thumb against his knee, distinctly more agitated than his companion. Finally, he could contain himself no more. "Okay, what exactly are you suggesting? That Annabelle will say no if I don't present her with the right flowers? Or if I don't say the right words? It's just a marriage proposal, you know. A simple question with a yes or no answer. I'm positive she'll say yes."

Babineaux turned slowly towards him, that fishing line tugging at his eyebrow again. He looked amused as if surprised to find the inspector still sitting there, let alone venturing to talk.

"I have a ring," Mike continued. "I'll pick a good moment, and I'll simply ask the question. That's all there is to it. People propose all the time. Not all of them are grand gestures. What are you trying to do? Make me think there's more to it than that? You're just trying to make me second-guess myself, Bambino. I'm not having it!"

Slowly, Babineaux set his cup down, uncrossed his legs, interlaced his fingers, and leant forwards across the table. As always, he placed a dramatic emphasis on his words by pausing before uttering them. "It iz not about ze yes or ze no, *Inspecteur*. You are right. She will say yes. Of zat, I am sure."

Mike tried to hide a smile. He felt relieved, but he didn't want the French detective to realise how much his words reassured him. "Good," he said. "I'm glad you agree."

Babineaux shrugged. "But it iz a shame, iz it not?"

Mike frowned some more. "What do you mean?"

"To a man," Babineaux said, pointing his finger in the air, "ze proposal is as you say, 'a yes or a no question.' Were it up to us, we would ask it at ze breakfast table, in between ze conversation about ze weather and ze latest football results, *non*? But to a woman . . . To a woman, it is an *event*, a *moment,* somezing to be remembered. It is a symbolic gesture of ze love up to zat point, a story to be told to friends and future children, a representation of everyzing she 'olds dear. Zis is how a woman zinks—in symbols and moments. You leave ze toilet seat up, it iz not a simple mistake, it iz a sign of how much you don't care about 'er. You buy 'er chocolates at ze gas station on ze way 'ome, it is not about ze cost or ze quality, it iz a symbol of 'ow much she is on your mind."

Mike found himself laughing. "That's rather stereotypical. And sexist. Annabelle would have your guts for garters if she heard you."

Babineaux chuckled, leaning back in his chair and opening his arms wide. "We are detectives, are we not? We, of all people, should know 'ow much truth zere is in ze stereotypes."

"I still don't need your help," Mike said, gulping down the last of his coffee and getting up.

"Zink about it, *Inspecteur*," Babineaux said. "When she tells ze story of 'ow you proposed, will 'er eyes light up and 'er 'eart skip a beat? Will she feel a warm glow, a deeply moving reminder of what a wonderful man she committed her life to? Or will she simply say: ''e asked me over dinner —I 'ad ze chicken'."

CHAPTER FORTY-TWO

ANNABELLE FOUND MARY in the convent's vegetable garden. She watched her friend for a few moments. Mary was digging furiously, turning over dark soil with a fork that was almost as large as she was. On the ground next to her was a bag of manure. Annabelle could hear Mary pant and grunt with effort and saw her wipe her brow before she plunged the fork into the dirt again. With a stamp of her foot, Mary thrust the tines in further and pushing down with her entire bodyweight, levered the soil up. She gave the fork an angry twist. Fresh soil dropped on the ground next to her, and the tiny nun raised the handle above her head, preparing to pitch it into the ground again.

"Mary! Yoo-hoo!"

Mary looked up. Annabelle showed her the two mugs she held in her hands. Her friend tossed down her fork and marched over to her.

"PG Tips," Annabelle said. "From a little stash I brought over with me specially."

"Thank you." Mary took the mug from Annabelle, gratefully wrapping her hot, pulsing palms around its sides.

"You look like you've been busy." Annabelle nodded to the bed that Mary had been working over. Half of it comprised dark, steaming, fresh soil whilst the other half was dry and compacted.

"I'm preparing it for planting. I'll work in the fertiliser when I've loosened up the soil. Bit of a smelly old job, but someone has to do it. And today, I felt like it should be me." Mary wiped her brow.

The two women strolled over to where an old wrought iron bench sat overlooking the vegetable garden. It was surrounded by overgrown shrubs and flowers left to grow wild.

"Hmm, what's that smell?" Annabelle lifted her nose to the air and closed her eyes.

"Mint, probably. From our herb garden behind you." Annabelle turned to see a profusion of plants, all various shades of green and distinctly different from one another. "Ah yes, I recognise the mint. And there's rosemary, and chives, and dill. And what's that? Cow parsley?" Annabelle pointed to a bush with tiny white flowers.

Mary turned to look. "Yes. Mother Renate likes a cup of cow parsley tea before bed."

"Huh, I thought cow parsley was a weed." Annabelle saw another patch by the hedgerow that ran alongside part of the vegetable garden. She turned back to Mary. "So what's got you into such a mood? I thought you were going to murder that soil the way you were stabbing it with your fork."

Mary immediately banged her mug down on the bench, sloshing her tea over the sides. She folded her arms. "I'm angry, Annabelle." She twisted in her seat. "I'm angry—

with God, with Raphael for disappearing, with myself. I don't know what to do."

"You are being tested, Mary."

Mary threw herself against the back of the bench, sloshing more of her tea. Annabelle took her hand. Her touch seemed to calm the nun. Mary closed her eyes and turned her face to the sun, exhaling deeply.

"Yes . . . yes, you're right. I'm in such turmoil. I want . . . *this* to be over. I keep waiting for a sign. I think I get one, but then another one, a contradictory one, pops up. Then some time goes by, and I get yet another sign. More contradictions. Oh, I'm just so confused. I don't know *what* is expected of me." Mary started to cry. "And I feel so ashamed."

"Ashamed? What do you have to feel ashamed of?" Annabelle was aghast. She reached into her pocket and pulled out a packet of tissues.

"I've broken my vows, Annabelle. To God. I have sinned."

"I'm sure it's not that bad, Mary. Tell me, you'll feel better if you do."

Mary shook her head.

"Is it to do with Father Raphael?"

Mary didn't reply. She stared down at her lap.

"Whatever it is, Mary, God will forgive you."

Mary nodded and started to blub again. Annabelle put her arm around her friend's shoulder and hugged her.

"Will you forgive me, Annabelle?" Mary said through her tears.

"Me? Of course I will, Mary. I'd forgive you anything."

CHAPTER FORTY-THREE

"IS THAT COLOGNE you're wearing?" Annabelle said as she sat down for breakfast.

"Um . . . just a little," Mike mumbled, shuffling in his seat as Annabelle took hers.

Annabelle closed her eyes and smiled warmly. "I like it." She opened her eyes again and appraised him. "You know, I think the French sense of style is rubbing off on you," she said.

"Really? How?"

"Those cufflinks for a start." Annabelle grinned.

"You don't like them?" Mike said, fingering the silver and blue cufflinks he'd bought at a jewellery store on the plaza the day before. He might have seen Inspector Babineaux wearing some very similar.

"No, I do like them. They're very stylish. Style makes you look even more handsome." Annabelle lifted her coffee cup to her mouth and wrinkled her nose flirtatiously.

Again, Mike tried to quell the small smile that threatened to telegraph his feelings. *Damn that Babineaux! His advice on women is as good as his investigative instincts are poor!*

"How did you get on with Inspector Babineaux after I left yesterday?" Annabelle plucked a croissant from the table. "You came back late. I was so tired when I returned from the convent, I went straight to bed."

"Oh . . . well . . . you know, we had a lot to go over—about the case, I mean. Babineaux prattled on a lot. We disagree on many things." Annabelle nodded, satisfied with his explanation. "How did you and Mary get on yesterday?"

Annabelle sighed. "Mary is having a crisis of conviction. It's quite common. She's not sure she's cut out for the sisterhood. We had a long chat."

"Huh, but hasn't she been a nun for years now? Why is she suddenly having second thoughts?"

Annabelle smiled. She leant over and ruffled Mike's hair. "Why indeed?" She didn't elaborate, and Mike decided not to probe further.

"We're over halfway through our trip now. We've only got a few more days left," he said, changing the subject.

"Yes. I'm still sorry this hasn't turned into much of a break for you."

"It's alright," Mike said, shrugging. "Even an investigation can be satisfying when I'm with someone I respect."

Annabelle's eyes widened. She smiled. "Respect? That's so . . . nice."

"That we spend time together is the main thing."

"You're right, that's the main thing."

"Annabelle," he said deliberately, causing her to raise her eyes from her croissant expectantly, "the French sunlight really brings out the beautiful shades in your eyes."

It wasn't quite what he meant to say, but Annabelle immediately went red and beamed. "*Mike!*" she said, reaching her hand across the table to take his. "What a sweet thing to say!"

"Just stating the facts," Mike said, gruffly.

"It's just so . . . unlike you." Annabelle retained her glow for several more moments. They continued to eat their croissants, Annabelle's eyes bashfully glancing at the inspector every so often.

Mike stared down at his plate. *Now?* Here they were, the bright yellow morning sun filtering through dancing leaves, the sounds of small birds chirruping their mating calls to one another, the smell of cherry blossom mixing with the rich buttery aroma of a delicious breakfast; it was perfect. Or at least, it would have been, were it not for the darkness of two deaths hanging over their thoughts like a heavy, velvet cloud.

"That's it!" Mike said, slamming his palm on the table, ruining the romantic mood, and causing Annabelle to snap to attention. "I'm going to solve this murder today! We've only got a few more days left, and I intend to enjoy them with you."

Annabelle leant back, her eyebrows raised. "How do you intend to do that?"

Mike's face was determined. "The pieces are all there: Julien and Renate's histories, the death threats, Raphael's disappearance. The one thing that bothers me, a hunch I never should have left hanging, was that sound at the church. I'm going back there, and I'm not leaving until I figure out what it is—even if it does turn out to be just some plumbing that's as old as the building. I'll ask Mary to come with me. She might have some insight I've missed." He bit off a mouthful of croissant like a lion tearing meat from a carcass.

Annabelle smiled, her face going red once again. "You

know, Mike, you're terribly attractive when you're determined to do something."

Mike looked up. He gave her his best thousand-yard-stare but found it rather difficult with his mouth full of soft, fluffy, buttery pastry.

CHAPTER FORTY-FOUR

WHEN MIKE ARRIVED at Babineaux's café-office, the French inspector greeted him with a wry grin. Before Babineaux could say anything or discomfort him further though, Mike took charge of the conversation.

"I'm going to investigate the church one more time. Sister Mary is going to join me there."

Babineaux's smile turned to a shrug of acquiescence. "Come, I will walk with you." The tall detective got out of his chair.

"I assume by ze fact you say nothing of it, zat my advice worked, *non?*"

Mike huffed a little. "Well . . . she noticed the cologne."

"*Bien!* Scents are very important to a woman."

"And the cufflinks."

"Ze details make ze man!"

"And she seemed to like those flowery words . . ."

"*Fantastique!* A man is only as good as 'is words," Babineaux said, misinterpreting the saying but making his point nonetheless.

"But I feel such a fool saying them!"

"*Mon ami!* Love is foolish! And to love is to embrace being a fool!"

"But there are still two massive problems," Mike said. "The first one is this bloody murder investigation. How can I be romantic when there's death and suicide and conspiracy everywhere?"

Babineaux offered a Gallic shrug. "We must do what we can," he said sympathetically. "What is ze other *problème?*"

Mike sighed and huffed as if needing to expel air before more words would come out. "I have no idea what to say!" he cried. "Complimenting her over breakfast is one thing, but asking her to be my wife is quite another!" Mike ran his hand through his hair. "I have to face it, I need help, Bambino, help!"

"Hmm," Babineaux stroked his moustache thoughtfully. "Come, come, *mon ami*. We will consider zis together. What does *Révérend* Annabelle like? What *moves* her? Is it music? Art? Poetry?" They were crossing the plaza now.

"Cake. She likes cake."

Babineaux raised an eyebrow and continued. "Well, we have plenty of zat 'ere. Sweet zings and sweet nothings make an excellent *combinaison.*"

Mike blew out his cheeks. Together, the two men noticed Sister Mary emerging from a side street.

"Do not worry," Babineaux said, patting the inspector's arm. "We will come up with somezing. Ze proposal will be sweeter zan any cake *Révérend* Annabelle ever ate!"

CHAPTER FORTY-FIVE

THE CONVENT FELT eerie as Annabelle traipsed up the worn path in the early morning light. She had decided to come back whilst Mary was gone to further probe the goings-on there. She hoped that Mary's absence might make the nuns open up more. Annabelle noticed a couple of black-clad figures silently conducting their work in the orchards and a nun hurrying to the barn, a basket in her hand. As Annabelle drew near, she noticed the stocky figure of Sister Josephine coming towards her.

"*Bonjour*," Annabelle said cheerfully.

"Good morning," the nun replied, her French accent making her English words sound complex and exotic. "Sister Mary isn't here at present. She left fifteen minutes ago."

"That's alright, Sister. I just came by to see how you were doing following Mother Renate's death."

"We are doing well, Reverend," Sister Josephine replied crisply. "Thank you." The nun bowed her head slightly. She seemed more reticent than the other day when she had been only too happy to dish on Father Raphael.

"Oh," Annabelle said. "That's good." She said nothing more. Sister Josephine looked at her expectantly.

There was an empty pause as both women waited for the other. Sister Josephine blinked first. "You are welcome to come inside, of course," she said. "Or you can wander around the grounds."

"Thank you. Is Sister Simone here?"

"Yes. But I'm not sure where."

"No problem, I'll walk around, see if I can find her."

Sister Josephine bowed politely and swooped off like a bird taking flight, her veil rippling like a stingray wafting through water searching for its prey. As she watched her, Annabelle was reminded again of what Sister Mary had said about the nun's coolness towards her.

Turning, Annabelle made her way to the big barn beside the river, where they milled the wheat and baked the bread. She pushed open the stout, aged-oak door and walked inside. The small vestibule was in darkness. It led to the milling operation in one direction and the bakery in another. Propped against one wall beneath some empty shelves, Annabelle could just make out a workbench.

"Baking must be over for the day," Annabelle murmured to herself.

Only a thin beam from a small high window provided any light, and just a square foot of the floor could be seen with any clarity. Annabelle groped for a light switch, but before she found it, the silence of the convent was broken. Annabelle heard a hard clang in the dark, the loud crash of something heavy falling followed by a low rumbling that got louder and louder. There was an enormous crash. A door burst open. Annabelle's eyes didn't need to adjust to realise there was something heavy thundering in her direction. She quickly leapt onto the workbench, banging her head hard on a shelf as she did so. "Aargh!" Ignoring her pain and lightheadedness Annabelle desperately perched herself on her hands and knees on top of the bench and squeezed her eyes tight. She felt a rush of air as something huge and heavy trundled past her. It was followed by another almighty crash and then silence.

Annabelle sat back on her heels and rubbed the spot on her head where she had hit the shelf. She waited for her heartbeat to return to normal. The outside door opened, and she squinted into the light. There was a flurry of moving figures silhouetted in the doorway. Alarmed voices spoke quickly in French.

Two nuns fluttered up to Annabelle and helped her down from the bench, whilst another propped open the door. Daylight filled the room—and shone a light on what had just happened.

"I am so sorry, Reverend!" one of the nuns said in English. "Please forgive us!"

"There's no light! The bulb is broken!" the other explained.

Still dazed and rubbing the crown of her head, Annabelle looked beyond the nuns at the giant millstone that had ended its journey by crashing into the vestibule wall. It had proved no match for medieval stonemasonry, however. It now lay in three pieces on the floor.

CHAPTER FORTY-SIX

"WHAT HAPPENED?" ANNABELLE asked drowsily.

"We were switching the millstones over. We use a pulley on the outside of the building," one of the nuns explained. "The handle slipped in my hand, and it got away from us. We're so sorry."

Annabelle gave them a wan smile through a slowly receding throb of pain. "It's alright," she said. "My fault. I should have let you know I was coming."

"Come outside," the nun said, gesturing for the others and Annabelle to join her. "Let me see the bruise."

Annabelle made her way into the daylight—almost blindingly bright after the darkness of the mill. Several pairs of hands compelled her to sit on an old bench against a wall whilst one of the women parted Annabelle's hair to look at the injury.

"Perhaps some tea?" the English-speaking nun suggested.

"*Oui!*" another replied. She scurried off.

A few moments later, an old wooden cup was thrust

into Annabelle's hand. Bits of crushed leaves sat at the bottom in yellow water. "Cow parsley tea. It's good for healing. Mother Renate, God rest her soul, used to swear by it."

"Thank you," Annabelle said. She was becoming bothered by the fussiness of the nuns. It was a bit early in the day for such a lot of attention.

"Drink."

Annabelle brought the cup to her lips. "Arghh!" A stab of pain shot through her shoulder. She flinched. The cup went sailing through the air. It landed a few feet away, spilling its hot contents onto the soil floor outside the barn.

"Oh!" Annabelle exclaimed, clutching her shoulder.

"Are you alright?"

"Yes, yes," Annabelle said, holding up her palm to protest against any further ministrations. "Just an old hockey injury flaring up. I'll be as right as rain in an hour or so."

The nuns nodded, shrugging and muttering in French. "Would you like some ice?"

"No, no, I'll be fine. But would you be so kind as to fetch Sister Simone?" Annabelle said, still rubbing her shoulder. "If she's free."

"Of course," the English-speaking nun said, quickly leaving. The other two stayed behind, watching Annabelle curiously from a few feet away as though she were an alien being of a kind with which they had had little contact. Which indeed, they had not.

"I'll be fine, really," Annabelle said to them. "Please, continue with your work." The nuns, getting the gist, wandered off wordlessly, and Annabelle sat for a while, raising her face to the sun and letting the warmth comfort her after her shock. She rolled her shoulder gently, easing away the dull ache, and gingerly brought her other hand to her head again. She felt the swell of the emerging bruise.

Sitting there, soothing her injuries, alone in the vineyard of a convent in a strange place, Annabelle felt, for the first time, out of place. What on earth was she doing? She had intended to have a pleasant—perhaps romantic—week with Mike, and instead, she was off on her own chasing a killer, maybe two. She loved Mary dearly and could never have said no to her request for help, but she wondered now if they could have helped in some smaller sense. Perhaps they could have left the thrust of the investigation to the appropriate authorities without compelling Mike to use his week off searching medieval churches for clues or requiring her to dance with death in a grain store.

Just as she was considering how she might show her appreciation for Mike's sacrifice, her thoughts were interrupted by Sister Simone. She appeared from around the corner of the building, squinting and wrinkling her nose like a mole who'd just breached the surface.

CHAPTER FORTY-SEVEN

"ANNABELLE, HELLO." SEEING Annabelle holding her head with one hand and rubbing her shoulder with the other, Sister Simone said, "Are you alright?"

"Sister Simone," Annabelle replied, getting up from the bench to greet her. "It's wonderful to see you again."

The elderly nun offered her right hand, but Annabelle grimaced and pointed to her shoulder. "Sorry," she explained. "I had a little accident."

"What happened?"

"Didn't the nuns tell you? A flying millstone almost flattened me!" Annabelle chuckled.

Sister Simone frowned and marched towards the open barn door, peering in to look at the aftermath. She shook her head almost imperceptibly.

"My fault," Annabelle explained. "I arrived unannounced."

The sister glowered at Annabelle. "No. The nuns know how to work a pulley. They've had lots of practice. I train them myself. They probably weren't paying enough attention to what they were doing. And what is this?" the elderly nun said, noticing the wooden cup on the ground. She picked it up and lifted it to her nose, immediately grimacing. "Ugh," she said, tossing what was left of the tea out towards the fields and placing the cup back on the bench. "Do you think you can walk? It will help if you keep moving. You won't become too stiff."

Sister Simone helped Annabelle up, and slowly they walked away from the building.

"The investigation is not going well?" Sister Simone asked.

"What makes you say that?"

"If you are back here so soon, you must have made little progress."

Annabelle couldn't argue with that. As they walked, they passed the large wooden shed. Most of it was surrounded by weeds, but the undergrowth had been beaten back around the door.

'Mary said you keep machinery, ropes, you know, 'shed things' in there."

"There? Yes, a whole lot of things we have little use for but which might be useful one day. We also store our surplus threshed wheat—the wheat we don't have room for in the other building.

"Can I take a look?"

"Of course!" Sister Simone reached to unlatch the heavy door.

"How have things been since Mother Renate . . . passed?" Annabelle asked.

"The only thing to live beyond death is a legacy," Sister Simone replied. "And Mother Superior's legacy was one of routine and obedience. The sisters have that still. We can carry on for a while until a new Mother Superior is appointed." Annabelle stepped into the dusty, dim interior of the shed whilst Sister Simone placed a rock in front of the door to keep it open. Slowly, Annabelle's eyes adjusted to the darkness, the small amount of light reflected a million times in the floating dust particles. The shed was as Sister Simone had described it—full of old, unused things. Curious, rusted machines; boxes and containers with layers of dust so thick they obscured the labels; a few old bicycles in the corner amongst a pile of wood, metal sheeting, and rope. Cobwebs bound them all together in a messy, angular parcel.

"Here's where we keep extra bins of threshed wheat," Sister Simone said, pointing to big plastic bins stacked on top of one another.

Annabelle peered at them. "So these are all full of grain?"

"That's right. When we need them, we bring the bins over to the other building to be milled."

Annabelle nosed about examining the other items but didn't find anything of particular interest. There were some old kitchen cupboards mounted on the wall. "May I?" Annabelle said, reaching a hand towards them.

Sister Simone shrugged her permission. Annabelle opened and closed all the doors, but the shelves were empty except for one. In the last cupboard was a bottle of molasses, some olive oil, and an old ice cream tub. Fingerprints marred the otherwise perfect layer of dust on the tub's lid.

"What's this?" Annabelle murmured. She lifted down the tub and opened it. It was full of soft, grey powder.

Sister Simone walked over. "That? That's rye flour. We haven't baked with that in years." She took the tub's lid from Annabelle and snapped it firmly back on. "I should throw it away." She tucked the tub under her arm. "Anyhow, does any of this help you?"

Annabelle looked around the shed and frowned. "Not really. The ropes . . ." she said, walking to the heaped pile that lay on the floor beside the bikes. "Presumably Mother Renate took the ones she . . . used from here."

"It would have been rare for her to come into the shed. She hated dust," Sister Simone said. "But yes, I suppose she must."

Annabelle prodded the ropes with her foot. "Do you really think Mother Renate killed herself?" she asked, more out of dead-end desperation than genuine curiosity.

Sister Simone pursed her lips. "I am not a fortune teller, unfortunately. I really couldn't say."

"But you must have an opinion?"

"Renate was a devout holy woman. She went by the book. Suicide would be anathema to her, and she seemed fine when I brought her tea that evening, but who's to say what was in her mind. That is between her and our Lord. We cannot know."

Annabelle sighed again. "Did you know there was a connection between Father Julien and Mother Renate?"

"Connection?" the old woman asked.

"They both came from Nice, miles away from here, and yet decades later, they end up in this tiny village together."

"Hmm," Sister Simone murmured. "I never had any idea. But I would say it is a coincidence. The world of all things holy is a small one these days."

"I know," Annabelle said. "But then Father Julien dies, and days later Mother Renate appears to hang herself. It's a bit, well . . ."

Sister Simone allowed herself a mild laugh. "You've been reading *Romeo and Juliet*, I see."

Annabelle matched the nun's chuckle. "There doesn't

need to be romance at the heart of it but . . . well, it was a thought."

Sister Simone shrugged. "I would be surprised if he were her secret."

"But you think she had one?"

Sister Simone paused, her face falling.

"What?" Annabelle said. "What is it? *Did* Mother Renate have a secret?"

CHAPTER FORTY-EIGHT

FOR A FEW seconds, Sister Simone looked at Annabelle, studying her, weighing her options. Eventually, she seemed satisfied and, after a deep breath, began talking.

"When I was a young novice, important considerations were not part of my experience. I liked to gossip, to giggle at saucy jokes, to play silly games. It took much more than a habit and a vocation for me to become worthy of God's love. One of the games I played with the other equally childish novices alongside whom I served the Lord in those early days was to guess the motivation behind other nuns' decisions to take their vows. Whilst we all say we are called by God, the stories behind our choices are often mundane and not at all spiritual.

"Many of the reasons are as you might expect. Some young women feel blessed by the Lord and seek to honour that. Others crave a sense of importance, of greater meaning in their lives. A few simply struggle to function anywhere else and want a place of safety. But sometimes, there's a more complex reason, a life-changing event, perhaps some trauma, or an illuminating experience.

"As I matured, I lost interest in those juvenile worldly distractions that had so held my interest. I stopped devouring magazines with handsome movie stars on their covers. I stopped lingering at shop windows full of glamorous clothes, and refrained from gossiping with the other nuns. But I could never stop wondering why my sisters had decided to take a pious path. It was an almost unconscious habit, a bad one. When I said my prayers and lay down to sleep, my mind would often drift, and I would wonder about a new sister I had just met. The reason for their decision would nag at the fringes of my mind, and I would speculate almost without realising it."

"And you think there's an extraordinary story behind Mother Renate's decision to join the church?" Annabelle asked.

Sister Simone sighed. "I have an idea." She quickly held up a finger. "I have no evidence, mind you."

"Tell me."

"I believe she may have had a child." Annabelle gasped, her hand jumping to her mouth as her eyes opened wide. Simone nodded at Annabelle. "And her shame and despair drew her to a life serving God."

Sister Simone sat on a grain bin and continued. "Over the years, I have noticed many things. There was a sad, longing look in Renate's eyes whenever there was talk of children—particularly girls. The only time you would see her smile was during visits by local schoolchildren; she insisted upon taking them around the convent herself. Her manner was quite different at those times. She was softer than normal. She even smiled. Her sorrow was most noticeable, however, when a child appeared on our doorstep."

"Lost?"

"Not exactly. One morning, we found a baby in a basket left at our door. Just a few hours old, it was. It doesn't happen much these days, but years ago it wasn't so unusual for unwanted children to be given up in this way, secretly left at the doors of a convent where the mother could be sure that their baby would be taken care of and raised in a godly manner, a life from which she may have fallen."

"How awful!"

"Yes. It was very sad, but with the Lord's blessing, we were usually able to make a childless couple very happy and give the child a home with love and consistency. Nevertheless, when it happened here, Mother Superior found the situation very difficult. She was distraught. I had never seen her like that. She couldn't be in the child's presence. She delegated the arrangements for the adoption to me. When it was time for the baby to leave, she spent three days locked up in her quarters praying obsessively. I would go to her door to bring her food, and almost every time I did, I heard the sound of weeping that would abruptly stop when I knocked. It was the only time I saw her feelings get the better of her."

Stunned, Annabelle breathed in deeply and shook her head in an effort to process what she was hearing. "And you think this was because she had had a similar experience years before? She had a child that she gave up for adoption? You think that's why she was so affected?"

"Maybe. Or the baby died." Sister Simone shrugged and stood up to wander to a shelf where she fingered some bottles. "Let's stop this talk. I am telling you what I observed, and I am speculating like I used to when I was younger. This is not useful, nor is it in the service of our

Lord. Come, let us leave here and turn our minds to other matters."

As she said it, there was a long, slow creak followed by a click. The shed went dark. Annabelle gasped, unable to see a thing. Her heart skipped a beat. She heard Sister Simone tut under her breath and the sounds of feet shuffling towards her.

"What's going on?" Annabelle exclaimed.

"The rock must have slipped from the door."

"But we can open it, can't we?"

Annabelle heard Sister Simone walk past her, then grunt a little as the door gave a tiny creak.

"The latch has fallen. We're locked in."

With her arms out in front of her, Annabelle moved through the darkness towards the sound of Sister Simone's voice.

"Careful!"

"Oof! Sorry," Annabelle said, bumping into her. "Do you have a lighter?"

"Good lord, no. I stopped smoking years ago."

"Matches? Candles?"

"No."

"Hmm." Annabelle ran her fingers over the door. "Perhaps we can yell for help?"

"These walls and the door are three inches thick. We are well away from the main paths. No one would ever hear us."

"I know! There's a sliver of light coming in. Perhaps we can slip something between the door and the frame? We might be able to lift the latch."

"*Bonne idée!*" Sister Simone exclaimed. "But we need something slim and some light to see by." There was a pause. "Wait!"

Annabelle felt the small, determined frame of the nun push past her.

"What are you doing?" Annabelle asked.

There was some rattling and clanging and a grunt. "There's a bicycle light here attached to the wheel by a dynamo, so if I just . . ."

Bright, white light flared, blinding Annabelle for a few moments until she caught sight of Sister Simone in the shadows. She was lifting a bicycle by its handlebars with one hand and spinning its front wheel with the other.

"Quick!" Sister Simone said, her voice tight with effort. "I can't do this all day!"

Annabelle sprang into action, her head spinning rapidly as she searched the cluttered shed for something thin enough to slip around the door. After picking up a piece of plywood and quickly discarding it for being too thick, she found an off-cut from a sheet of aluminium and rushed over to the door.

"Does it fit?" Sister Simone asked, struggling under the weight of the bike and the awkwardness of her task, the bicycle light flickering as she grew tired.

Her answer was a click. Annabelle slid the aluminium into the crack around the door and pushed it up to dislodge the latch. The door popped open, first a little and then a lot, as Annabelle leant her shoulder, her good one, against it. Then, misjudging the effort required, the door burst open. Annabelle pitched forwards, tumbling onto the ground outside.

"Ow!" she cried as she hit the dirt. Despite her pain, she stood up quickly and held the door open for Sister Simone before allowing the door to slam shut again under its own weight.

"What's going on, Sister Simone? I doubt that rock

moved by itself," Annabelle said, rubbing her shoulder. Now she had injured them both.

"I agree with you," Sister Simone replied, scanning the outside of the shed. "It is very odd."

CHAPTER FORTY-NINE

MIKE, BABINEAUX, AND Mary marched up the church steps like they were superheroes. There was a sense of purpose about them, the English detective spearheading the group, the other two trailing slightly in his wake. Mike was frowning, his lips pressed into a thin line, hands thrust into the pockets of his trench coat. They stopped at the doors. Lestrange who was trotting behind, stepped forwards to unlock them. Silently and respectfully, they crossed the threshold. They began to move around the immense space, taking slow, deliberate steps between the pews and carefully scanning the walls around them as if they had never seen them before.

After Father Julien's death and Father Raphael's disappearance, there had been few visitors to the church. Without services, confessions, and random prayers, it hadn't taken long for the church to feel disused. As if yearning for its past, the church felt like a relic and the effect on the visitors was profound.

"There's nothing sadder than an unused church," Mary

said softly, almost to herself. Nobody responded, their silence agreement enough.

Not one of them failed to notice the small changes in the church's interior since Father Julien's murder. Spiders had been busy weaving large cobwebs in its nooks and crannies, the pews had a sprinkling of dust along their dark oak surfaces, the air was as musty as that of a crypt.

Halfway up the aisle, Mike stopped and turned around to face the other three, his eyes fixed keenly on Mary. "Okay," he announced, with the voice he used to command his officers. "Tell me again what happened that day. From the top."

Mary nodded quickly and began. "We were all here for Easter Sunday Mass . . ."

"We?"

"The nuns, the entire village, and those who live in the countryside around."

"Where were you specifically?"

Sister Mary turned to the pews on the left-hand side of the church. "Here, near the front, on the same side as the office."

Mike looked at the spot she pointed to, envisioning the scene. "Where was Father Raphael at this time?"

A quick blush flashed across Sister Mary's face. "He stood by the door, waiting for Father Julien."

"I see," Mike said. "So you could see him clearly from where you sat?"

Mary flushed again. "Yes."

"What happened after you arrived?"

"Well . . . Father Julien came out and walked to the altar. He had his back to us as he prepared to conduct the service. He liked to look everything over, to check everything was in place. There was nothing unusual about any of it."

"Father Raphael was still standing to the side?"

"Yes," Mary said. "The music started, and everyone went quiet. The service was about to start. That's when Father Julien turned around, took a step, and . . . fell. Everyone gasped. We were stunned! Sister Josephine started screaming. Sister Simone was quietening her. Mother Renate ran up the aisle. I looked back to where Father Raphael had been standing, but he had gone!"

"Hold on," Mike said, raising a large palm. "Sister Josephine started screaming?"

"Yes!" Mary said, confounded by the inspector's question. "Father Julien was dead!"

"But you didn't know that—not yet," Mike replied. "All he'd done was fall over. He could have fainted or had a heart attack. He could have simply tripped over. Bit of an overreaction to start wailing straight away, isn't it?"

"*Inspecteur*," Babineaux interjected. "She is young. Of course ze young woman was distraught. Even if 'e did, as you say, 'trip over.'" The Frenchman shook his head slowly and muttered something that sounded to Mike suspiciously like *"Ze British and zeir upper stiff lips . . ."*

"Perhaps," Mike said, putting the point aside but not conceding it. He looked at the door to the office, screwed his face up in thought for a second, and then marched towards it. The others quickly followed. "So Father Raphael was standing here, right?" Mary nodded.

"Father Julien walks past him towards the altar," Mike said, moving his hand as if pushing an imaginary Father Julien in that direction, "then everyone waits for the Mass to start."

"Yes," Mary said.

"We 'ave gone through zis a million times," Babineaux sighed.

"So everyone was looking at Father Julien," Mike continued. Abruptly, he spun around and pushed open the door to the office, stepping inside quickly as the others filled the doorway behind him. Mike's eyes went immediately to the small, head-height window. There were two bars across it. Mike grabbed one firmly, shaking it a little before turning back to Mary. "Tell me, could Father Raphael have gone through this window?"

"It iz too small!" Babineaux said, causing Mike to scowl at him.

Sister Mary considered Mike's question for a full four seconds before answering. "He's very athletic and slim . . . but . . . perhaps. I don't know."

"Okay," Mike said. "I'm going to dismiss the window then."

He marched out of the office, the others quickly moving aside to let him pass before filing in behind the determined inspector once he had done so. After a few steps, Mike stopped abruptly. His companions banged into him and each other.

"Father Raphael couldn't have moved from his post *into* the church," Mike said, recovering quickly and ignoring the others as they straightened their clothes and hair and rubbed their bruises. "You would have seen him. That leaves only one way he could have gone."

Quickly, Mike moved down the side of the sanctuary to the front of the church, one palm brushing against the wall until he came to another door. It was hidden by a velvet curtain that matched the red carpet that ran down the aisle. Mike pushed the curtain aside and rapped his knuckles on the door behind it. "What's this door?"

"It leads to the confessional," Mary answered.

"Why is it so small?" The door was at least six inches shorter than was typical.

Mary turned down the corners of her mouth. "Discretion? Age? People were smaller in the 15th century." Mike glanced at Babineaux.

"*Lestrange!*" the Frenchman cried. He held out his hand and clicked his fingers without taking his eyes off Mike.

CHAPTER FIFTY

LESTRANGE STEPPED FORWARDS, plucking the heavy bunch of keys from his pocket and trying several until he found the right one. Beyond the door, they found themselves in a tall, wide, but short corridor. At the other end was another small door, and to the side, a couple of ornately-carved booths. Mike stopped a few feet into the corridor, taking in as much of it as he could.

Here, the space was different. The walls had wood panelling, and the floor was made of varnished oak slats. Another narrow red carpet ran down the centre. Babineaux walked past Mike, brushing his moustache as he peered at the confessionals like an art critic, one hand behind his back.

"This other doorway?" Mike said, his eyebrows high on his forehead. He pointed to the door at the other end of the short corridor.

"It's for people who want to slip in and out," Mary answered. "Anyone can confess during certain hours or at a prearranged time. They can enter here from the alleyway behind the church. It's much more discreet."

Mike nodded and took a few careful steps forwards, scanning the room. "Mary," he said slowly, his eyes still steadily considering his surroundings.

"Yes, Inspector?"

"Does the church have problems with its plumbing?"

There was a pause before Mary spoke. "I don't think so. How do you mean?"

"Noises. Rattling. You know, the kind of sound you get when plumbing is old. Air gets in the pipes."

"Noises? Not at all. I often come to the church to just sit and contemplate. It's one of the most profoundly quiet places I know. Even when there's a market or some kind of fair in the plaza, if the doors are closed you would think the church was in the middle of nowhere."

"Hmm," Mike said, frowning. "What about this?" He pointed to a recess built into the wall. There were three more, but this one was different. It was empty. Each of the others contained an artefact stored inside a glass case—a box, a goblet, a clock—all of them antique, ornate, and gold. On the wall was a large piece of artwork depicting *The Last Supper*. "Why is this one empty?"

"Oh!" Mary exclaimed. "It's missing! I hadn't noticed." She walked up to the blank spot in the recess and stared, as if by doing so, she could conjure up the missing item.

"What is? What's missing, Mary?"

"St. Agnès. Her remains are stored in a tall gold box, and kept behind this glass. The box is missing!" Mary turned to look at Mike, her eyes wide with horror. "This is terrible. They are sacred!"

Suddenly, they were distracted by the sound of the two

French policemen talking animatedly. Babineaux was waving his hand at Lestrange, dismissing him.

"What is it?" Mike asked, walking over to them.

"Nothing! Lestrange used to be a carpenter's apprentice —'e iz obsessed with wood!"

Mike looked at Lestrange. He was pressing his foot slowly but firmly on a spot in the carpet. Mike crouched down quickly, gesturing for Lestrange to move out of the way. He grabbed the carpet and flung it aside. There, set into the floorboards, was a small iron ring. Mike didn't even look up to get the reaction of the others before yanking at the handle.

"Mon Dieu!" Babineaux said, peering into the black hole that appeared.

"Anyone got a light?" Mike asked.

Lestrange opened his roomy jacket, and like a magician pulling a rabbit from a hat, he produced a torch. Mike quickly put the end of it into his mouth and slid himself through the opening. He let go of the sides, and a second later, the sound of his shoes landing on the hard stone reverberated around the walls. Babineaux, Mary, and Lestrange knelt to peer down into the hole, their mouths open, waiting for the inspector to tell them what he could see.

"My God!"

"What iz it!?" Babineaux shouted excitedly into the cellar.

"There's a man down here!" came Mike's startled response.

It took a second or two for things to click, but when they did, strong instincts took over. Mary hitched up her habit and leapt into the hole, her skirts acting like a parachute, her veil like a sail. She landed lightly on the stones below. She ran towards the beam of light, slamming into the inspector.

"What are you doing, Mary?" Mike exclaimed.

"Where is he?" Mary instructed, her voice gruff and uncharacteristically low. Mike cast the torch's beam to illuminate a dirty thin figure slumped against the wall in the corner of the chamber.

"Oh!" Sister Mary wailed as if days of hurt and pain were being experienced all at once. She threw herself down next to the figure, who rolled his head at the sight of her. "Raphael! Raphael! You're alive!"

The young man raised a weak smile. He looked a sight. His lips were chapped, his face gaunt. Dust had mingled with tears to leave his skin streaked with dirt. And yet, despite his suffering, it was still possible to make out Raphael's chiseled cheekbones and strong jaw—the handsome features that had paraded along the catwalks of Paris. Mike shouted up to Babineaux and Lestrange. "Water!!" he yelled. "Quickly!"

Once again, after some rummaging, Lestrange and his jacket came to the rescue. He passed a bottle of water to Babineaux, who tossed it down to Mike.

"He must have been here since everything kicked off. He's in pretty bad shape," Mike said to Mary, crouching next to her and handing her the water. "Look, he's been knocking on the pipes with that piece of wood. That was what I could hear."

"Raphael," Mary said, "drink this." She gently tipped the water between his parted lips. The man closed his eyes as the cool liquid moistened his dry mouth.

"It's alright," Mike said, gently pressing a hand on Raphael's shoulder. "We're here now, and you're alive. We'll get you to a hospital."

"What iz 'appening?" Babineaux's voice wafted into the cellar from the trapdoor. "Iz everyzing okay?"

"Yes!" Mike said, standing up and walking back to the opening to see the long oval face of the French detective peering down at him like a moon. "We've found Father Raphael. It looks like he's been trapped here since the murder."

"*Sacré bleu!*" Babineaux cried. "We must arrest 'im!"

"Are you insane?"

"It iz ze perfect crime! 'e killed ze priest and 'id 'imself away where no one could find 'im!"

Mike rubbed the bridge of his nose and shook his head. "For crying out loud, what are you talking about? Get a doctor, you fool!"

Mike looked at the couple on the ground. Mary was kneeling on the floor offering Raphael some more water. She was tenderly wiping his face with a white handkerchief. "I'm so sorry, Raphael . . . I've thought so much about what you said . . . I haven't thought about anything else. And then, I thought you were . . . The answer's yes. Of course it is! Yes, Raphael! I will marry you. Nothing would make me happier! I'm just so sorry I had to say it like this! Please forgive me for making you wait so long!"

Mike's eyes widened. He almost dropped his torch. *Father Raphael proposed to Sister Mary? How can a half-dead priest who's spent days trapped in a cellar be doing better than I am?*

CHAPTER FIFTY-ONE

THAT EVENING, WHILST Father Raphael recovered at Doctor Giroux's cottage hospital, Sister Mary a constant presence at his side, Annabelle, Mike, and Babineaux ate dinner together at Chez Selwyn. On the way to the restaurant, Mike had told Annabelle about Mary's acceptance of Father Raphael's marriage proposal. Annabelle had smiled serenely. "I'm sure they will be very happy," had been her only comment.

The meal lasted five hours, and everything about it was intense and passionate. Only a third of the time was spent eating. The rest was spent debating, talking over one another, and occasionally listening to various points and counterpoints. Halfway through, even Mike began gesturing with his hands. At tables around them, their fellow patrons ate in silence, listening intently to the talk of murder, conspiracy, and other nefarious acts until, towards the end of the night, they too had formed their opinions and began to argue amongst themselves.

"It doesn't make *sense*," Annabelle said, waving a piece

of wine-infused beef on the end of her fork. "Why would Father Raphael lock himself up in a secret cellar?"

"But do you not see, *Révérend*," Babineaux answered, opening his arms wide imploringly. "To make 'imself look like ze *perfect victim*."

"No," Mike said gruffly, shaking his head. "You're wrong. You saw the rug placed over the trapdoor. Father Raphael couldn't have got himself down there *and* pulled the rug into place."

Babineaux shrugged and waved Mike's comment away. "A passerby, or ze nuns, perhaps—zey see ze rug, zey fix it! You are focusing on ze details *too* much!"

"He nearly *died!*" Annabelle exclaimed through a mouthful of beef.

"Not every criminal iz a competent one," Babineaux replied quickly. "Maybe 'e intended to 'ide and zen found 'e couldn't get 'imself out of ze predicament 'e got 'imself into."

"You've been barking up the wrong tree from the start, Bambino," Mike said.

"I do not know what zat means—but I assume by your tone, it iz not a compliment," Babineaux said, with a tilt of his head. "If not ze Father Raphael, zen who? You are very good at dismissing my instincts, and you 'ave spent much effort in exonerating ze priest," Babineaux admonished from behind a waving finger. "But you 'ave offered me no other suspect. So I ask you, if not ze Father Raphael, who? Me? Ze waiter? Ze ghost of Moriarty?"

Mike sighed and looked at Annabelle, deferring to her. She furrowed her brow.

"Father Julien and Mother Renate had a connection . . ."

"Oh! Again with ze *connexion!* We do not even know if

ze Mother Superior was murdered! It is still officially a suicide, *Révérend!*" Babineaux said, stopping as Mike glared at him to allow Annabelle to finish.

"And I've been thinking. What if . . . what if they had a child together? A child they gave up for adoption before Mother Renate joined the church."

"*Sacré bleu!*" Babineaux said, fanning himself with a napkin. "And you accuse *me* of fairytales. You are going from A to P to Q and back to A again! *Révérend!* I must say, ze English seem to 'ave a better grasp of concocting mysteries zan zey are at solving zem!"

"But you see, today I was at the convent, asking questions. Strange things kept happening. Dangerous things. Things designed to scare me, put me off, even harm me. Someone didn't want me there. I don't think that convent is the pure, devotional, holy place it is purported to be. I think they are hiding things."

"*Quelle imagination! Imaginations fantastiques!*" Babineaux scoffed.

"Are you alright? Are you hurt?" Mike asked. This was the first he'd heard of Annabelle's challenging day. He put a hand on her arm, his eyes full of concern.

"I'm fine. But it was disconcerting. I think we need to look further into the goings-on there."

"Zere iz another possibility . . ." Inspector Babineaux said slowly.

"Oh? What other possibility is that?" Annabelle asked.

"Well . . ." he began before stopping himself and sighing heavily.

"Go on! What is it?"

"*Révérend*, you know 'ow I respect you. I 'ave seen many times 'ow intelligent and insightful you are . . ."

"What are you on about, Inspector? Please, spill the beans!"

"Somezing else I do not understand, but I zink you mean me to 'urry up. One person brought you 'ere with ze sole purpose of exonerating Father Raphael. Ze same person who does not get along with ze other nuns. Ze same person who keeps inviting you to ze convent where strange zings 'appen to you."

Mike looked at Babineaux, then back at Annabelle. He fiddled with the stem of his wine glass.

"Inspector, you can't . . . !" Annabelle was breathing so heavily her shoulders rose and fell despite the weight of Mike's heavy hand he placed there to calm her. She opened her mouth several times to start speaking but couldn't find words to express herself. After one more deep breath, she finally said in a strangled voice, "I have known Mary since I was a baby."

"Iz she loyal? Would she do anyzing for you?"

"Of course!"

"Zen I imagine she would do just zat for Father Raphael too. She is madly in love with 'im."

Once again, Annabelle found herself stunned into silence. "I can't believe what you're saying," she said eventually, shaking her head vigorously.

"We cannot ignore ze facts. Inspector Mike keeps saying so."

"You think Raphael killed Julien, and that Mary has been protecting him all along?" Pink spots appeared on Annabelle's cheeks.

Babineaux pursed his lips and turned down the corners of his mouth. He gave a little shrug and crossed his legs. He placed his hands, crossed at his wrists, over his knee. "Maybe."

"Mary would never be involved with anyone who had committed such a terrible crime."

"Perhaps you don't know your friend as well as you zought. Before you arrived 'ere, did she tell you she was in love with a priest? Zat 'e 'ad proposed marriage to 'er?

"Well, I . . ."

Babineaux tapped the side of his nose. "It iz best to keep an open mind, no?"

"Well, yes, but . . ."

"Zen we shall. We will open our minds, and," Babineaux leant towards Annabelle, smiling now, "our 'earts."

The three diners went back and forth long into the night. The sun set over the church, and eventually the only light left was the flickering candles at the table and the old-fashioned lamps that hung in the church square.

After a dessert of cheesecake topped with figs and honey (Annabelle had seconds) and unable to agree on anything at all, they took their leave of one another. Sufficiently comfortable now, having drunk enough wine, they did so in the traditional French way—with kisses on both cheeks. Even Mike submitted.

CHAPTER FIFTY-TWO

THE NEXT MORNING, Annabelle was first to breakfast. She felt discouraged as she rifled amongst the books looking for something to pass the time whilst she waited for Mike. She eventually settled on an English magazine and got stuck into an interview with the star of a British period drama winning awards on both sides of the Atlantic. Annabelle quickly became engrossed. Claude brought her some coffee and pastries. "Would you like some eggs, *Révérend?*" he asked her. "Or cheese and some freshly baked bread?"

Annabelle looked up from her magazine and beamed at him. "Yes, please."

When he had gone, Annabelle stared across the lawn, her interest in her magazine taking second place to her thoughts. Babineaux's comments about Mary the previous evening were gnawing at her. Not for one moment did she believe that Mary had anything to do with Father Julien's death, but Babineaux was right about one thing. Mary had kept a secret from her. A big one. And whilst Annabelle understood why Mary had done so, it made her heart break just a little.

Annabelle gave herself a silent talking to. Over time, things changed. Alliances shifted. That's just how it was. They weren't young girls anymore. They were adults with big grown-up issues to navigate. Annabelle shook herself and picked up her magazine again. Claude returned as Annabelle was flicking through pages trying to find the conclusion to her article.

"Claude, you've been here since . . . ?"

"1964, *Révérend*."

"So since before Father Julien arrived?"

"*Oui*, our previous priest died. He was very old. It was rumoured he was over a hundred."

"Gosh, that is old. So you first met Father Julien what, sixteen years ago? That's when he took up his post here, isn't it?"

"Oh no, I met him for the first time several years before that. He was doing construction work in the village. He moved on to become a priest and later returned here to serve the Lord. He always said he liked the village so much he found a way to come back. Many people feel that way about this place." Claude wrinkled his forehead as though he couldn't understand why.

"Interesting!" Annabelle looked at the tray Claude was carrying. "What examples of heavenly deliciousness have you brought for my breakfast today?"

Claude didn't smile at Annabelle's playfulness. Claude never smiled. Solemnly, he recited the tray's contents. "I have cheese soufflé, warm fruit compôte, pain au chocolat, ham, and cheeses with some rye bread."

"Rye bread?"

"*Oui*, it is particularly good with the ham. Did you see a pig as you went about?"

Annabelle thought back to her first stroll around the village. She nodded.

"Well, you won't see it anymore."

Annabelle shut her eyes for a long moment. "That's nice, how very . . . rural."

"Rye was Father Julien's favourite bread. He had some every day." Claude deposited the food on the table and shuffled away. Annabelle ignored the ham. She pressed some brie onto the bread and took a big bite.

She chewed slowly, her thoughts turning to the case and her experiences of the past few days. She felt forlorn. Guilt for dragging Mike on this trip to nowhere, a feeling of sorrow around her altered relationship with Mary, and frustration that there was still no solution in sight to the mystery of Father Julien's murder. She gave a great sigh and pressed more brie onto her bread.

"What's up?" Mike said when he arrived a few minutes later, finger combing his wet hair into a semblance of order. Annabelle was flicking the pages of her magazine back and forth furiously. Finally, she slapped it onto the seat of the chair next to her. "I do hate it when they do that."

"What?"

"Put the end of an article at the back of a magazine where you can't find it. Never mind, it's nothing."

Mike sat down and forked a piece of ham onto his bread. "Listen, I forgot to tell you last night what with all the kerfuffle about finding Father Raphael and Mary, and . . . you know. Anyway, before we found him, we discovered that a gold box containing the relic of St. Agnès is missing. It's normally kept in a recess in the back room where the confessionals are, but it's disappeared. Mary said this was a big deal. Is that right?"

"It is. I wonder where it might have gone."

"Who would want such a thing?"

Annabelle thought. "I can't imagine. People used to believe that relics were capable of performing miracles, many still do. It's not that unusual."

"Hmm, they're not short on unusual people in this village, that's for sure. But maybe the relic wasn't the target. Would the box have been valuable? If it was stolen, the thief might have taken it for its resale value and not have known about the relic."

"Then they'd get a nasty surprise when they opened the box."

They heard footsteps, and Mary appeared around the corner of the auberge.

"Mary!" Annabelle cried. "How lovely to see you. What are you doing here so early?"

CHAPTER FIFTY-THREE

"MORNING, ANNABELLE, MIKE. I'm so sorry to interrupt your breakfast," Mary said, wringing her hands. "But I thought you'd want to know as soon as possible."

"It's fine Mary," Annabelle said, rubbing a hand on her friend's arm. "What is it? Not more bad news? How is Father Raphael doing?"

Sister Mary took a few breaths and nodded. "Better. He's in a state of shock—delirium. Doctor Giroux says he'll sleep it off, and with plenty of rest, he should be fine in a few days."

"That's good to hear," Mike said.

"And how are *you* doing?"

Mary gave a little smile. "I'm fine. Lots to do, you know. People to tell. But that's not really what I came to say," she said, growing anxious again. "Raphael woke up—only for a brief moment—but he said something."

"What?"

"He just said . . . It was ever so strange . . . '*The nuns*'."

"The nuns?" Mike repeated.

Mary nodded. "I wanted to ask him more, but I didn't want to stress him, and he fell back asleep right away. It could have been a dream or something . . . I don't know. Annabelle, Mike, you don't think it could mean that . . . well, um, the nuns put him in there? Down that hole?" Annabelle sighed sympathetically and looked at Mike.

"After what happened to you yesterday . . . all those 'accidents' . . . " Mike said to Annabelle. "What do you think?" Annabelle knit her brows and waggled her lips back and forth as she thought.

"I should go back to Raphael," Mary said. "I just thought you'd want to know."

"Okay, Mary, we'll see you later," Annabelle said, patting Mary's arm before she hurried away. "Oh! Mary! Wait!" Sister Mary stopped and looked back at them. "Just out of curiosity, are there any nuns in the convent that are in their mid-twenties? Twenty-four or twenty-five?"

Mary brought a finger to her lip as she considered the question. "I'm not sure . . . Véronique, perhaps. Sister Josephine, for sure. Her birthday was just last month. I don't think there are any others. Not that I can think of off the top of my head, sorry." Mary left, leaving Annabelle and Mike to look at each other with thoughtful expressions.

"That was an interesting question," Mike said. "Why did you ask that?"

"Just something I've been thinking about."

"And . . . ?"

"It's just wild speculation. I have no evidence, and I know how you are about evidence." Annabelle was idly spreading more brie on her bread. It was thick and creamy, and she left butter knife marks in it as she pressed down.

"Alright, but you clearly have a theory."

Annabelle sighed and put down her knife. "Claude just

told me that Father Julien worked in the village before he was a priest. He did some construction here."

"Okay."

"Well, that would put him in the village when Renate was at university in Reims not too far away. It strengthens the idea that there was something between them."

"And you think if Mother Renate did have a secret child, that child, now grown, might be at the convent?"

Annabelle shrugged. "It's a possibility."

"But why would you think that?"

Annabelle leant on the table, her shoulders slumped. "No reason, just my fanciful imagination. You're right. And really, if Renate and Julien did have a child, why would the child track them down by pretending to be a nun? I'm just letting my imagination go wild. Too many romance novels, I suppose. Forget I said anything. It's a silly idea." She picked up her butter knife again and started bouncing it on top of the brie. It made a pleasant thumping sound.

"Interesting that Sister Josephine is the right age, though," Mike said.

"How so?"

"I had a thought when I was at the church yesterday. Mary said that as soon as Father Julien fell to the ground, Sister Josephine started crying."

"That's plausible."

"Not really," Mike said. "All he did was fall. Everyone was shocked, yes, some people rushed to his side—but to just start crying? No one could have known he was dead at that point." Annabelle's eyes widened. "What is it?"

"What if Father Julien and Mother Renate were in a relationship whilst she was at university and he was working in the village. She found out she was pregnant and went to Switzerland to have her baby. After secretly giving up her child, she entered a convent, perhaps out of shame. And then that child sought them out. A child seeking to wreak revenge on those who abandoned her!"

Mike huffed the way he sometimes did when he considered a possibility that had huge ramifications. "Perhaps you *have* been reading too many romance novels."

"That's what you said before about Mary and Raphael. And I was right then." Mike didn't respond. "Do you think we're getting warm?" Annabelle prompted.

"Well, it's a theory, certainly. But . . ." If he was honest, Mike thought the reality of this was about as likely as him adopting Babineaux's grooming habits. But this was Annabelle talking . . . He grabbed her hand. "Oh, come on. There's only one way to check it out. Let's go!"

CHAPTER FIFTY-FOUR

IN A CLOUD of dust, Annabelle drove the Mini to the convent. Her hands and feet pounded and pummelled her gearstick, brakes, clutch, and accelerator as she manipulated them all with the coordinated skill and precision of a rally car driver whilst Mike held on to the dashboard, eyeing Annabelle warily whilst being shaken to a frenzy from which he wondered if he'd ever recover. When the convent buildings came into view, the car skidded to a halt on the loose dirt. Annabelle turned the engine off sharply and was out of the car in a flash. Mike matched her for timing and pace even though he didn't quite know where Annabelle was headed.

The sounds of doors slamming caught the attention of a nun who seemed to have a cold. She blew into a handkerchief as Annabelle called to her, waving.

"Hello? Sister Colette?"

The nun glanced around anxiously before trotting over to them. "*Bonjour?*" she said. Her nose was red, her eyes watery.

"Hello," Annabelle said, once again, trying to smile through her panting.

The nun gave Mike a quick glance before looking away. "*Pardonnez-moi, s'il vous plaît,* no men allowed," she whispered to Annabelle.

"That's okay," Mike said, quickly offering a placating palm. "Is Sister Josephine around? Perhaps she can come out to talk to us."

"Josephine?" the nun said. Behind her, the bakery truck emerged from the back of the convent and rumbled slowly past them.

"Yes. Josephine," Annabelle said. "Here?" She pointed to the ground and then to her open mouth. "To talk?"

"Josephine? No, Josephine not here," the nun said, her eyes anxiously moving to the departing truck.

Mike tugged on Annabelle's arm. "Annabelle," he said.

"Hold on, Mike." Annabelle pulled her arm away and looked at the nun. "When will she be back? Erm . . . *Quando . . . Ici . . . Zurück?*"

On hearing a French word amongst two unrecognisable ones, the nun launched into more than a few sentences of fast, complex French, replete with gestures, shrugs, and even a little giggle at the end.

"*Pardonnez moi, mais . . .*" Annabelle stuttered as Mike continued to watch the truck speed up as it trundled down the track.

"Annabelle, I think . . ."

"Mike! Please! Erm . . . *Quelle heure . . .*" Annabelle said, tapping her watch in front of the nun. "Josephine come back *ici?*" she said, making swirly gestures with her hands before pointing down at the ground.

The nun continued to talk in complicated, frenetic French. Annabelle didn't understand a word.

"Annabelle!" Mike barked suddenly. "She's in that truck!"

Annabelle looked behind her quickly to see the vehicle crest the brow of a hill and disappear. She looked at Mike, then at the nun, and back to Mike again. "Blast!" she cried. She sprinted to the Mini.

Annabelle had the car in motion in seconds, the inspector flailing to close his door as she reversed. After she'd spun the Mini like a pro, she revved the motor as they zoomed down the dirt track away from the convent.

"Are you sure?" she shouted to Mike over the noise of the roaring engine.

"I don't understand French, but I understand body language—and that nun was stalling," came Mike's reply. He held onto the dashboard again, this time for dear life.

As they sped along, they passed Babineaux and Lestrange lounging next to their 2CV parked on the side of the track. Lestrange watched them drive by whilst Babineaux leant against the car, smoking a thin cigar.

Ignoring them, Annabelle pressed on. She caught sight of the truck just as it reached the end of the track. To the right was the road that led to the village. To the left was the wood and, beyond that, the interconnecting network of roads that led to the rest of France. The truck turned . . . left.

Annabelle sped up. She took the turn with the inch-perfect racing line of a Formula One driver and gained plenty of ground on the truck just before it turned a corner and disappeared from view. Annabelle raced to the corner and threw the car into it. With a deft flick of her wrist, she dropped down a gear, almost without slowing. Mike braced himself against his door and the dashboard. He correctly anticipated a fearsome pull of gravity as

Annabelle negotiated the adverse camber of the road surface.

She turned the car so sharply that the Mini rode on two wheels for several yards before righting itself, causing Mike to suppress a shout of fear that they would tip over. Once all four wheels were back on the ground, they looked ahead for signs of the truck, but it was nowhere to be seen. It had disappeared. Annabelle slammed on her brakes and stopped the car, their seatbelts the only thing keeping Mike and her from flying through the windscreen.

"Where did they go?" she said, scanning the horizon.

"There's only one way *to* go. They are heading for the main road. She's escaping!" Mike replied.

Annabelle didn't need to be told twice. She plunged her foot down again on the accelerator, causing the Mini to shoot forwards, not thinking twice now about two-wheeling it around corners in pursuit of the truck. Her sole focus was to chase it down the long, rough road that was the only way into—and out of—Ville d'Eauloise. And yet, despite her efforts, when they reached the hill that led up through the woods, the truck was a mere dot disappearing into the shadow of the dense trees.

"Damnit!" Mike said as Annabelle built up momentum to attack the hill. "By the time we reach them, they'll be gone!"

Annabelle answered by gritting her teeth and pressing harder on the accelerator. "Not if I have anything to do with it!" she cried as the car powered up the hill. "My Mini is a nippy little thing, and we can catch up to a rumbling old truck, no problem."

Annabelle gripped her steering wheel until her knuckles were white. If she could drive the car up the hill using nothing but her determination, she would. She pinched her lips and her eyes narrowed with effort. The road was still rough, and she and Mike bounced up and down inside the small car like a couple of pieces of popcorn at the bottom of an empty bag, but they were too focused to be concerned. With their eyes fixed ahead, they slipped under the canopy of the oak trees. There was no sign of the truck. They ploughed on.

"Look!" Annabelle said.

"What? I don't see anything!" Mike cried.

"Exactly! We should be seeing the truck. It's disappeared. Where's it gone?"

Mike peered around. In the distance, amidst the oak trees, he saw the truck lumbering away from them, weaving around tree trunks and fallen branches as it attempted to get away. "There!" he pointed. "It's gone off-road."

Annabelle spun the steering wheel and once again set off after the truck. As she eased her beloved car cross-country, wincing as she jolted the underside against debris and rock, another vehicle appeared amongst the trees ahead of them.

"Don't tell me they've got an accomplice!" Mike exclaimed just before he bashed his head on the car roof.

His answer came quickly. With driving skills that impressed even Annabelle, the other vehicle approached the truck from the side, gained speed to overtake it, and then dramatically swerved in front to cut it off. It slid sideways, cutting lengthwise across the truck's path, causing the driver to slam on the brakes. It stopped mere inches from the other vehicle as Annabelle's Mini pulled up and pinned it from behind.

"It's Babineaux!" Annabelle exclaimed.

"Well, well, well . . ." Mike said.

But it was not Babineaux who quickly and purposefully

got out of the driver's seat, whipping out his police badge and wielding it in front of him as he walked to the truck. It was Lestrange.

By the time Annabelle and Mike clambered from the Mini, two nuns had climbed out of the truck and were remonstrating loudly with the sergeant. Inspector Babineaux was slower to emerge. His door flung open and after two long seconds, he staggered out of the 2CV groaning slightly, his burgundy three-piece suit creased and dusty in a way that obviously displeased him.

CHAPTER FIFTY-FIVE

ANNABELLE AND MIKE jogged towards the fracas. As they ran up, Babineaux yelled in French at Lestrange who yelled at the nuns, who yelled at both of the policemen seemingly indiscriminately. Annabelle suspected that even a fluent knowledge of French wouldn't help her understand what on earth was happening. The four furious French people were so passionately engrossed that they barely noticed the two English visitors.

"Everybody!" Mike shouted in his most commanding crowd-control voice. "Calm down!" His tone was loud and forceful, causing them all to spin around and stunning them into silence. "What the hell is going on here, Bambino?" Mike said.

"Lestrange has gone mad!" Babineaux said, throwing his hands up in the air and then gesturing down at his dirty trousers as if they were proof of his sergeant's compromised mental health. "We were sitting on ze side of ze road one second, and ze next second, 'e seizes ze car! I tried to stop 'im, but all I could do was jump in ze passenger window! 'e starts driving through ze fields and through ze trees! 'e drove through ze forest with my legs dangling on ze outside! 'e could 'ave killed me!"

Babineaux glared at Lestrange, who quickly began explaining himself in French. His superior officer was having none of it, and off they went again gesticulating and explicating.

"One at a time!" Mike shouted, stopping the chaos before it got dug in too far. "What's Lestrange saying?"

Lestrange launched into a monologue neither Annabelle nor Mike could understand.

"Oof!" Babineaux cried out. He threw his hands up in the air and walked off a short way, his hands on his hips. "'e iz crazy! 'e iz talking nonsense!"

"But what is he saying?" Annabelle asked insistently.

Babineaux took a deep breath, looked at Lestrange, who was still talking, then turned back to the English visitors.

"'e says zat when 'e saw ze truck leaving ze convent, 'e knew somezing, 'ow do you say, was *up*. Zat zey 'ad no reason to leave today . . ." Babineaux paused as Lestrange continued to talk. "'e says 'e 'as been observing zeir delivery schedule and zat since Mother Renate died zey 'ave not produced any new batches of bread, and zat zere is no reason ze truck should be leaving . . . Zen 'e says zat . . . *Mon Dieu*! But it is too *stupide*!"

"Tell us," Mike growled.

With another sigh and a melodramatic shrug of his shoulders, Babineaux continued. "I am sorry to translate such idiotic zings—even in translation, I feel a fool for letting zem pass my lips. My sergeant says 'e zinks ze nuns are 'iding somezing. Zat . . ." Babineaux stopped to laugh, rub his face, and shake his head despairingly. "Zat you were chasing zem, so 'e thought 'e would 'elp. *Quelle bouffon!*" He turned to glare at his hapless sergeant.

Mike and Annabelle exchanged a quick glance. "He was right. We were chasing them," Annabelle said.

Babineaux's eyes widened with shock before he slapped a hand to his face and looked up to the heavens imploringly.

"We think Josephine might be the love child of Father Julien and Mother Renate and that she murdered both of them as revenge for abandoning her," Annabelle informed him.

Mike raised his eyebrows, his eyes widening fractionally at Babineaux who looked at him incredulously, man to man, detective to detective, for confirmation. Mike looked down at the ground briefly. Suddenly, there was a clanging at the back of the truck. The gathered group moved as one to stand behind it as the doors swung open, revealing the figure of the nun hiding there.

"Véronique!" Annabelle cried.

The young, shy nun, the aspirant trying on the sisterhood for size, looked out at them. She was no longer dressed in her demure clothes but in a pair of jeans and a pink t-shirt. There were tasseled, suede ankle boots on her feet. She looked no less beautiful than earlier, but there was a serious, hard expression on her face as she stepped down from the truck with the grace and poise of a queen descending her throne.

Her audience was speechless. Véronique stood in front of them, her shoulders back, chin raised, proud and defiant. All traces of the hesitant young woman she had been were gone. "Very well," she said, her voice firm. "I suppose this is the end."

CHAPTER FIFTY-SIX

IT WASN'T THE most conventional place to conduct an interview. In fact, it wasn't conventional at all. They had considered the office of Doctor Giroux, but with Raphael recovering there, it had seemed inappropriate. Annabelle had suggested the auberge, but eventually, they settled upon Babineaux's 'office' after the café owner agreed to shut the blinds and close for several hours whilst they interviewed Véronique.

At a round table in the corner, a single lamp above them illuminating it, Véronique sat with her back to the wall, her hands clasped in front of her, her back ramrod straight. Detective Babineaux and Annabelle sat opposite her, whilst behind them, Lestrange and Mike leant against the café counter.

Babineaux had changed his creased, dusty suit for a fresh, navy-blue pinstripe and felt all the more composed for it. With a flamboyant flourish, he plucked his phone from his pocket, set it to record, and placed it in the middle of the table.

"For ze benefit of our foreign friends," Babineaux said,

gesturing to Annabelle, "please conduct zis interview in English."

"Alright," Véronique said, swivelling her eyes to Babineaux whilst keeping her head fixed forwards in an upright, regal position.

"So, I assume you wish to confess," Babineaux announced, "and I suggest we begin with your death threats to Father Julien. Ze motive behind zem."

Without flinching, Véronique said, "I don't know what you are talking about."

"You wish to pursue zis charade? We found you in ze back of ze truck, I remind you. Dressed in . . ." Babineaux waved at Véronique's clothes, *"vêtements civils."*

"I wished to run away from the convent," Véronique said. "I didn't like it there. I do not want to become a nun. That is my confession."

There was a pause. Annabelle and Babineaux exchanged apprehensive glances.

"Véronique," Annabelle said, putting her hand on the table between them as if offering something, "as an aspirant, there's no need to run away. You weren't being kept there against your will. Simply notifying Sister Simone would have sufficed. Something else is going on."

Annabelle was interrupted by a haughty snort of derision. *"Ridicule,"* Véronique said.

"It's only a matter of time before we find out, Véronique," Mike said wearily, walking over. "I know you want to keep your dignity, but you're not doing that by delaying the inevitable."

"I am being dignified because I'm innocent!" the young woman said angrily.

"Listen to me," Mike said crossly, "you can confess now, and your sentence will probably be lenient. But if you don't, you will certainly be punished harshly. DNA tests will be run to confirm your parentage. Fingerprint testing will be performed on the death threats. Searches of your room will be performed for traces of the poison and the glue used in the letters. Interviews will be conducted with the other nuns, and the chances are that at least one of them will tell the police everything. But even without that, we will dredge up enough evidence to convict you during a trial. It will be long, painful, and humiliating for you—so I ask you to do this for your own sake. Confess and face the consequences under an umbrella of truth, rather than fighting hopelessly."

Véronique's head turned by only a few degrees, her green eyes—now so obviously reminiscent of Mother Renate's—piercing the assembled congregation.

"Quite a speech," she said. "I imagine it would work—*if* I were guilty."

Mike sighed loudly and went to the counter to grab a coffee. "This could last well into the night."

"Very well," Babineaux said slowly, stroking his moustache, "if you do not want to tell a story, I shall tell one myself. Let's presume ze first zing you ever knew was ze inside of an adoption centre. Was it an expensive one? Or a poor one?" Babineaux dismissed his idea with a flick of his wrist. "It doesn't matter because, of course, soon a family took you. 'ow could zey not? So beautiful! With such *belle* green eyes and thick raven 'air. Such a sweet *bébé*! And zey spoiled you, indeed. You bear all ze signs of a girl flattered. Look at you!"

Véronique's nose twitched. Everyone noticed it. Silently, Mike brought over his coffee cup leaving the saucer on the bar. His shirt sleeves rolled up, he sipped from the cup slowly as he watched what was unfolding.

Annabelle leant her forearms on the table, her hands clasped.

"You do not bear ze subdued manner of one who 'as been bullied," Babineaux said with a wry smile and a wave of his hand. "*Non*, rather, you 'ave ze cunning way with ze words and ze self-control of one who iz a very clever bully 'erself."

Véronique cleared her throat and looked away. Babineaux glanced at Annabelle, smiling and giving her a quick wink before continuing. Véronique shuffled her shoulders, her face tense. The French detective had taken away her one defence. He could see under her skin.

"But to 'ave everyzing only reminds us of ze one zing we are missing, does it not? For you, zat was your birth parents. You were so wonderful, so *special*. 'ow could zey abandon you? *Alors*, 'ow zat question must 'ave burned! Was zere somezing wrong with you? Somezing you did not realise? A young girl growing up must lie awake every night wondering such zings. Ah! But zere was an answer! You just needed to find zem.

"But 'ow did you do zat? No doubt through a *combinaison* of your charm, beauty, and intelligence—information, 'ints your adoptive parents gave you. You came to zis small village, tucked away in ze valley of ze French countryside, to find zat both of your parents 'ad become leading figures in ze church! Ze gall! Ze audacity! Two people who 'ad committed ze terrible sin of abandoning you were now masquerading as pure devotees of ze good Lord! But *ma cherie!* Why did you simply not tell zem? No doubt zey would 'ave taken you in zeir arms and expressed ze love for you zat you felt you deserved?"

Véronique's face contorted into an expression of disgust. "I would have spit on their *love*! They are not worth the ground they will rot within!" Annabelle sat back in her chair in the face of this sudden vitriol. Véronique was clearly done holding back.

"Yes! I hated them! And I am not sorry they're dead. And you may condemn me for it, but they tossed me aside like some unwanted gift. How long did they suffer? The priest, hardly at all? Mother Superior, a few seconds? *I've* suffered from the moment I was born!"

"But Véronique," Annabelle said slowly. "You could have shouted a bit, even thrown some things. Why did you have to kill?"

CHAPTER FIFTY-SEVEN

VÉRONIQUE PURSED HER lips, her chest rising and falling with hot breath, her eyes closed until she eventually spoke, her words hard-edged and taut.

"I didn't kill anyone!" She pointed at Babineaux. "He's right! It *was* outrageous for them to claim to be so holy, so divine. I would have preferred it if Julien were a criminal and Renate a drunk; I could have understood then. I would have been able to explain why they abandoned me. But they were upright, thriving, and devout. Nothing was stopping them from raising me as their own—nothing but their own selfishness.

"I came here, and every week I would watch Julien lecture people on serving the Lord, on morality, on doing good in the eyes of God—all whilst he had committed the sin of abandoning me to an unknown life. And Renate? Mother Superior? Ha! It's ironic to call her that, isn't it? To see her, every day, commanding the other sisters, telling them what to do, acting like the ultimate wise woman, a voice of supreme guidance. And yet she couldn't, wouldn't, face censure and raise a tiny, defenceless baby. She was a coward, for shame. She *sickened* me. But I was simply curious. I wanted to find out about them. I posed as a wannabe nun, so that I could see them up close." Véronique grabbed a glass of water from the table and gulped hungrily from it as the others exchanged glances.

Annabelle tried a different tack. "What about Father Raphael being found in a cellar in the church? Did you have anything to do with that?"

Véronique laughed, seeming to relish the explanation of her deeds as if reliving them. "Do-gooder Father Raphael," she said slowly. "Always in the way. So pure, so perfect, so respected. But he was dishonest, too. Just like the others. I saw how he looked at Mary. I saw them in the orchard once. I heard them professing their love for one another. They were just as bad as Renate and Julien. Lying, cheating, dishonest. Yes, I had something to do with that. But it was just a bit of fun."

"Bit of fun? He would have died if Mike hadn't found him!" Annabelle cried.

Véronique shrugged. "But he didn't, did he?"

"How?" Mike asked. "How did you trap Father Raphael in the cellar?"

"Perfect planning, of course," Véronique said as if they were merely making small talk. "I knew that all eyes would be on Julien at the front of the church as he said Easter Mass. I told one of the nuns to call Raphael to the confessional booths the moment Julien went to the altar. The nuns did whatever I asked and believed anything I told them. They were in thrall to me, so naïve, so gullible. A few stories, some chocolate, and a magazine or two, and they are anybody's. The nun told Raphael a story about noises coming from the cellar. The silly man trusted her enough to go down there himself. You can guess the rest. It was just a coincidence that Julien chose that moment to die. I knew you'd find Raphael eventually."

Annabelle shook her head and looked away as Babineaux let out a brief sigh of disgust. Only Mike kept his eyes steadily on the young woman.

"And what of Mother Renate," he said. "What do you have to say about her death?"

Véronique shook her head. "She was no loss. No one will miss her. The other nuns hated Renate almost as much as I did. Do any of you even know how much of a slave driver she was? Sometimes the nuns would only sleep three hours a night. She would have them doing the work of farmhands in the daytime, expect them to pray half the night when they were almost dead from heat and exertion, and then they had to get up in the early hours to bake bread! If she was killed, take a hard look at the nuns. Renate was a control freak. A tyrant."

"I guess that's where you get it from," Mike said, smartly.

Véronique ignored him. "I also enjoyed making things difficult for you too, *Révérend*, but you were a slippery fish."

"The millstone," Annabelle said slowly. "Locking me in the shed."

Véronique shrugged and chuckled lightly to herself. "You were just too good. Pitiable attempts, I know, but that's what you get for telling those thick-headed nuns to 'think' for themselves. They couldn't think if their lives depended on it. All they can do is follow orders, routines, and daily devotions. Spare me." Véronique looked at her nails and gave them a quick buff on her T-shirt before fixing Annabelle again with her emerald green eyes. "Listen, I may have played around, but I didn't kill anyone."

"I don't believe you," Babineaux said. "I zink it was time for you to make a stealthy departure from Ville d'Eauloise before our investigations led us to you," he added. "You figured zat if you left quietly, you would 'ave been long gone before we knew about it. Zat was why you were in zat truck."

Véronique sat back and folded her arms. "You are quite wrong, Inspector. I wanted out and knew that if I left publicly I would be subject to a whole lot of questioning that I didn't have the patience for. I decided to slip away. It was easy to convince the nuns I was the victim, and they offered to help me. Once Renate was dead, they were rudderless. They were as I believe the English call it, 'putty in my hands.'"

"I don't believe you." With one final, dramatic gesture, Babineaux reached over the table, turned off the recorder, and secreted his phone into his pocket. "I 'ave 'eard enough!" he said. He turned to Lestrange and said something in French, prompting the sergeant to take out his cuffs and lock them over Véronique's wrists. Babineaux got up. "Take 'er away and charge 'er!"

"With what?" Annabelle asked.

"Conspiracy, kidnapping, attempted murder! And we shall zink of more, no doubt. You may be beautiful *mademoiselle*, but zere is no beauty in your 'eart. And 'ow you got those nuns to 'elp you, I will never know." Babineaux flicked his head, dismissing the young woman. Lestrange led Véronique away.

Babineaux sat back and slapped his thighs, exhaling as he let the tension of the interview evaporate. With a clap of his hands, he made a proposal. "Shall we take afternoon tea, *Révérend*? I zink we are done 'ere."

When there was no reply, he looked over. Annabelle

wasn't paying attention. She was scrolling on her phone. Suddenly she grabbed her purse and her car keys and ran outside. Once again, Mike and Babineaux found themselves watching Annabelle race to her car. A moment later, all that was left in her wake were exhaust fumes.

CHAPTER FIFTY-EIGHT

"WHERE IS SHE going?" Babineaux cried out.

"I don't know, but wherever it is, she's not going there for fun," Mike replied. They ran to the 2CV.

"*Allez, allez!*" Babineaux cried out to Lestrange. The sergeant stopped reading Véronique her rights and looked up. After a moment's indecision, Lestrange handcuffed Véronique to a lamppost and jumped into the car after the other two men.

"I bet she's going to the convent," Mike cried from the back as Lestrange turned sharply away from the plaza and up the hill out of the village. Mike was hanging on to the back of both front seats as he tried to prevent himself from being tossed about like lettuce in a salad. When, oh when, was he going to get a decent ride?

Lestrange drove the car as fast as he could along the road to the convent in time to see Annabelle climb out and run into the big stone barn next to the convent.

"What should we do?" Babineaux asked Mike.

"She won't want us following. She would have taken us with her if she did. But she might be in danger." Mike hesitated for a second. "Let me go. I'll see what's what and step in if I have to." He sprung out of the car and ran to the barn, quickly opening the door and slipping inside.

He looked around. There was no sign of anyone, but in the distance, he heard voices, women's voices. They were low, calm, quiet. He tiptoed towards them and flattened himself against the wall next to a doorway. Peering around the doorframe, he could see Annabelle sitting at a table. Her back was to him, obscuring the person to whom she spoke.

"Tell me what happened. I know it was you who poisoned Father Julien. But I don't know why." Annabelle shifted in her seat, and for a quick second, Mike caught a glance of who sat on the other side of the table from her. Sister Simone!

"You poisoned him with that spoiled rye flour, didn't you?" Annabelle spoke sympathetically. "From the tub in the shed. You knew it was toxic and that over time, in small amounts, the stress on his body would eventually kill him. You essentially tortured him. Why did you do it, Simone? Why, after all these years of being faithful to the Lord, did you feel the necessity to take a life? And in such a way? How did it feel knowing that he would be steadily poisoned without realising that this elderly nun who went out of her way to bake him his favourite rye bread was really intent on killing him?"

"It wasn't terribly difficult. Julien was a vain man and a glutton." Simone spoke softly. Mike could hardly hear her. "He wouldn't question why I might bake him, and only him, a loaf of rye bread several times a week for months on end. He wasn't very bright either. He probably assumed the bruising on his arms and legs was the result of clumsy knocks or old age. His creaking joints, arthritis. The sore throat that came and went, the result of a virus." Sister Simone took off her glasses and gave them a polish before putting them back on. "But it was his heart that was my target, literally and figuratively. I knew it would give out in the end. It took time and patience, but the plan worked perfectly. It wasn't my intention for him to meet our Lord during Easter Mass, but it was as good a time as any."

"But why? Why did you do it?"

Simone nodded sadly. She looked at the table she and Annabelle were sitting at, examining the cuts and knots and the burns on its surface. "They were very discreet and clever, but I knew. They didn't know I knew, but I saw them together after Mass one evening. Renate was laughing. Renate never laughed. I knew then."

"And you didn't approve?"

Mike saw Simone flash an angry look at Annabelle. "Of course, I didn't approve. I couldn't stand it. I hated them both. There's a very fine line between love and hate, Reverend, and I couldn't distinguish between the two. They had broken their vows. I saw no reason why I shouldn't too."

"So you hatched this plan to poison Father Julien?"

Sister Simone had a mug of hot tea in front of her. The nun had her hands clasped around it. She twisted the mug between them. Mike could see steam rising from it. "I just wanted to hurt him at first, but as time went on, I couldn't stop. I became obsessed with him. I knew the fungus would kill him eventually, but I didn't care. I wanted him to die. With Julien gone, I thought my path would be clear."

"Clear to what?"

"To Renate, of course.

"Renate?"

"Yes, Renate. Dear, sweet, sad Renate." Tears welled in

Simone's eyes. "I loved her from the moment I saw her. I faithfully served her all these years. She was my soulmate. Don't you see, I could have made her whole again? I would have wiped away her tears for that spawn of hers, given her anything she wished for. Nothing would have made me happier than to devote myself to her for the rest of my life. But she wasn't interested. After Father Julien died, I told her how I felt . . ." Sister Simone faltered and looked sadly down at her mug. "She laughed. I lost my mind. That's when I decided to deliver the same fate to her."

"You poisoned her with the tea?"

"I brought it to her before bed that evening, except I switched her usual cow parsley for hemlock. They look almost identical, you know? Yes, of course you do. That's why you're here, isn't it? You are very astute, Reverend."

"I learnt that at one of Jessica Sparrow's bushcraft talks in my village. Never thought it would come in useful."

"I kept a small bush of it in one of our hedgerows, separate from the cow parsley in our vegetable garden. Anyhow, it was very quick. The hemlock caused respiratory failure, suffocation basically. It was easy to disguise as a hanging. Once she was dead, I lay her on the floor, tied the rope around her neck, and another shorter one on the hook above the fireplace.

"But *why* did you make it look like suicide?"

"To throw you off. Or at least to throw off those idiot policemen. I knew they would think she'd killed herself and not pay attention to the tea. I didn't think you'd be so stupid, but they outnumbered you and delayed things for a while. You were right. Renate would never have killed herself."

"So you found out that Father Julien and Mother Renate were having an affair, so you set about poisoning Father Julien with the rye bread. You hoped people would believe it was a heart attack, and then when you told Mother Superior what you'd done and why you'd done it, you killed her with hemlock tea and made it look like a hanging?"

Sister Simone sighed. "Yes, that's right." She twisted the mug in her hands again. "I don't regret it, you know. There was always going to be someone in pain, no matter what. At least now, they are together in God's arms for all eternity. Renate is finally at peace. Killing her was my final kindness."

"What about God, about love for him?"

"God? He left me years ago."

Mike shifted his weight and hit a small stone with his shoe. It made a clinking sound.

"You can come out now, Mike," Annabelle called. And then, more quietly. "It's all over now."

Sheepishly, Mike appeared around the doorjamb. Annabelle stood to face him. Sister Simone blew her nose and drained the dregs of her tea.

"I think Sister Simone is ready to face the consequences of her actions," Annabelle said.

There was a gurgle behind her. Mike's face froze. Annabelle whirled around to see the elderly nun slump over the table.

"The tea!" Annabelle cried. She leant over to shake Simone, but it was too late.

CHAPTER FIFTY-NINE

"ZAT IS ZAT, zen. A most intriguing case," Babineaux said.

"A horrific one," Mike said.

"A tragic one," Annabelle added. They had returned from the convent to Chez Selwyn for a debrief, leaving Sergeant Lestrange and Doctor Giroux to process the tragic scene of Sister Simone's suicide.

"'ow did you know it was Sister Simone, *Révérend*?"

"I must admit, I thought at first it was Véronique, but after she denied she was the murderer, it all fell into the place. First of all, the bread. Rye poisoning was common in the Middle Ages. The rye would develop a fungus and if eaten, would cause bruising, twisted limbs, and ultimately death. It was called *St. Anthony's Fire* back then. Sister Mary, or Mary as I should call her now, told me about a crop that was destroyed by the nuns after being contaminated with fungus. And later, I found a tub of rye flour in the shed. Sister Simone said they hadn't baked rye bread for years, but she was lying. There were recent fingerprints all over the tub. Everything in the cupboard was thick with dust, but the dust on the tub was smudged."

Babineaux nodded. "Clever, *non?*"

"And as you know, I couldn't believe that Mother Renate killed herself. For one, it would be against her beliefs, and two, her desk was a mess. She was such an orderly woman she would never have left it like that. I would have expected a note, too. But the clincher was that Sister Simone brought tea to the Mother Superior on the night she died. Cow parsley and hemlock look very similar, but one is harmless, beneficial even, and the other is deadly. But when I realised the murderer had to be Sister Simone, I was stumped. I couldn't think of a motive."

"So you went to track 'er down to get it out of 'er," Babineaux said.

"When I went to the convent, I thought that if I put what I knew to her, she might unburden herself. I think she had had enough of all the lying, death, and chaos. She knew the game was up and had decided confession and death was the only way forward for her. And so it was."

After dinner, the three of them left the restaurant and walked into the cool night air, the sun having long disappeared. The orange-tiled roofs of the buildings that were lit up in daytime were now in shadow. Daylight had been replaced by the warm glow of the moon and supplemented by street lamps that reflected the jewel-coloured stained glass of the church in pools of light that lay directly beneath them.

Babineaux sighed. "Sometimes, I zink zat a criminal is just a normal person with a twisted outlook," he said.

"It is often the case, Inspector," Annabelle responded solemnly.

"But we still don't know who was ze poison-pen writer," Babineaux said sadly.

"I would have a chat with Claude if I were you," Annabelle said.

Babineaux's eyes widened. "*Non!*"

"Ask him why pages are missing from his magazines."

"Well, I'm going to leave that one up to you, Babineaux. I'm finished thinking about criminals," Mike said as he stretched, his arms aloft. "I've got one day of my holiday left, and if you don't mind, I'd like to completely ignore the existence of crime for the duration of it."

Babineaux nodded graciously. "A fond farewell zen, my English detective friends. It was a pleasure to work beside you. I must admit without your 'elp it would have taken me a little while longer to solve zis mystery."

Annabelle and Mike exchanged smiles with the Frenchman. "Good luck, Inspector," Mike said, offering his hand.

Babineaux shook it and then embraced Annabelle with a kiss on both cheeks. "*Révérend*, it was a unique and delightful pleasure."

"Likewise," Annabelle said.

"Maybe we'll see you again before we leave," Mike said.

"Quite so," Babineaux replied, smiling broadly.

CHAPTER SIXTY

IF THE DAY had been long and chaotic, the night was dark and ethereal. Annabelle was exhausted. Arms intertwined and in comfortable silence, Annabelle and Mike walked up the hill to a bench that overlooked the village. Neither of them needed to say a word, their relief evident as they strolled slowly through the cobblestone streets. They passed a few villagers walking in the opposite direction who nodded at them as they passed, unaware of the dramatic day the pair had had.

"Well," Mike said, as they reached the bench, "I suppose we'd better find something to do tomorrow, or we might get bored."

Annabelle chuckled and leant her head tenderly on his shoulder. "I'm so sorry we ended up spending your week off running around investigating gruesome murders."

Mike wound his arm around Annabelle's shoulders. "I keep telling you, Annabelle, it's quite alright. That we've spent it together is enough. And we've had some good times, haven't we? We certainly gave that old man at the church something to talk about."

Annabelle looked up at him, a mischievous glint in her eye. "Perhaps we could go wine tasting or find someone to give us a French cookery lesson," she said with a wink. "Perhaps Welsh Selwyn would do it. Or we could go roaming around the beautiful countryside on bikes."

"As long as there aren't any chickens on the back." Mike nodded approvingly, then quickly frowned as he foraged in his jacket pocket. He pulled away from Annabelle, patting himself down hurriedly, then frantically. "Damnit! I don't have my wallet."

"Are you sure?"

"I had it in the restaurant. My police badge is in there!"

"Oh no!"

"I'll go and get it."

"I'm coming with you," Annabelle insisted. "I'm sure it'll still be there. No one in this quaint little village will pinch it."

They stood, re-threaded their arms, and began walking back the way they had come. It wouldn't take long. It was downhill all the way. As they neared the plaza, a low humming rose into the air around them as if the atmosphere were vibrating melodically.

"That's strange," Annabelle said.

"What is?"

"That sound. I thought I was imagining it at first, but I'm not. There must be a particularly deep, sonorous wind chime somewhere."

"Must be," Mike replied. They turned another corner.

"Do you hear it, Mike? Now sounds like human voices, a choir!"

Mike turned to her and frowned, straining to hear. "Oh yes, I can hear it . . . vaguely. Oh well, I suppose they're just practicing."

"Hmm." Annabelle lifted her face to the moon. "It sounds lovely."

"Yes," Mike said. "It does."

"Reminds me of St. Mary's. Makes me a little bit homesick."

At the end of another bumpy, narrow street, the plaza came into view. "Oh!" Annabelle exclaimed as she noticed people filling the square. A glow surrounded the crowd like a warm halo. Every single person was holding a flickering candle. "Something's happening! Look! What do you think it is?"

"It looks like some sort of ceremony."

They walked over to the crowd in front of the church. Old wrought iron lanterns lit the steps up to the church lighting up baskets of flowers linked together with large ribbons. A red carpet strewn with purple petals led up to the door of the church that had been decorated with a huge arch of white and purple flowers. Children wearing red cassocks sang a psalm, their pure high voices ringing out in the still night air. Annabelle slowed her pace as if she were entering a dream. The voices and the flames of the many candles seemed to make the air shimmer with hope and expectation.

As Annabelle and Mike got closer, the crowd in the square noticed them. Every head turned to the couple. Annabelle stopped and gasped, bringing a hand to her mouth as she noticed them looking at her and smiling. Mike took a step forwards before looking back at her.

"Is this for me?" she whispered.

CHAPTER SIXTY-ONE

MIKE REACHED FOR Annabelle's hand and led her forwards, the crowd parting to create a path that led to the church steps.

Wide-eyed and stunned, Annabelle allowed Mike to lead her through the crowd, the people closing in as they passed them. There was no escape from what was about to come. Annabelle noticed the faces around her, smiling, their eyes glittering with excitement. There in the crowd was everyone they had met in the past few days.

Babineaux tilted his head as they walked past. Lestrange said something in French. Sister Josephine peered through her thick glasses. Mary seemed to have tears in her eyes, and beside her, Raphael leant on a walking stick, beaming happily, much of the colour having returned to his face. Even Selwyn's elegant daughter, Françoise, was there.

At the bottom of the steps, Annabelle looked up to see a small table set in front of the church door. It was draped with a red cloth and decorated with more purple and white flowers. Mike and Annabelle walked up the steps towards it before turning to face the crowd, which was, by now, entirely still.

For a moment, they looked at each other, Mike smiling, slightly tense, and Annabelle still in a state of shock. She was unsure about what was to happen, but quite certain it would be momentous. The choir came to the end of their psalm and stopped singing, leaving a delicate quiet hanging in the cool night air.

Annabelle's eyes were fixed on Mike as he took a small box from the table and brought it carefully in front of him. He opened it slowly. Once Annabelle found the strength to peel her eyes from his, she looked down to find a glorious shimmering diamond ring sparkling like the stars in the sky, its light hypnotising her further.

Mike gracefully got down on one knee, proffering the diamond ring in front of him. He looked up at Annabelle, who clutched the crucifix she always wore with one hand as though it might hold her up if her knees failed her.

"Annabelle," Mike said, his voice low and tender yet seeming to flow through the clear, light, cool air, "every second I spend with you makes my world come alive. Before I met you, I felt as if there was nothing more for me to see and nothing more for me to do. The world seemed full of darkness. But then you made me laugh, you showed me joy, you gave me a new lease on life, you showed me a whole new world. You taught me what true love is. You are a wonderful woman, worthy of far more than I could ever give you, but I want to promise that I will do my best, that I'll never stop doing my best to make you as happy as you have made me. I love you, Annabelle. Will you marry me?"

During this speech, Annabelle's eyes got wider and wider. Her hand went to her open mouth. Her eyes slowly moved between the sparkling diamond and the inspector's bright, eager expression. Seconds passed. Everyone, from the youngest babe in arms to the most wizened, world-weary elder, was fixed upon Annabelle, their faces full of hope. In those seconds, dry lips were licked, heads craned forwards, breaths were held.

"Annabelle?" Mike whispered.

At the sound of his voice, Annabelle started. Slowly, she removed the hand from her mouth, a realisation dawning on her face, her mouth breaking into a huge smile. Her eyes welled with joyful tears. "Oh, Mike! Yes! Yes, of course! Of course, I'll marry you!"

The next moments were chaos. Annabelle threw herself at Mike who, rising quickly, caught her just in time to grab her in a tight embrace. The choir started singing "Hallelujah," the children's voices full of light and hope as they threw handfuls of rose petals over the couple, their high young voices offset by the deep baritone of Selwyn Jones, who had sprinted up the steps to join them. The crowd cheered and then applauded before their claps morphed into chants of *"Les Anglais, Les Anglais,"* as Mike and Annabelle turned and waved to the crowd.

In the excitement, everyone missed Babineaux giving Lestrange a quiet, discreet nod. But they didn't miss the rockets of bright colours that began shooting into the air above the church shortly thereafter, crackling and exploding into incandescent flecks of trailing, swirling, soaring light. The crowd cooed and gasped as the display continued, colouring the night sky in a rainbow of patterns and fire. Annabelle and Mike parted to cast their eyes overhead, transfixed by the flashes of coloured lights that glowed against the darkness.

"Oh, Mike," Annabelle said, as she again leant her head on his shoulder, "how on earth did you manage all this?"

Mike chuckled lightly. "I had a little help," he said, casting his eyes down onto the square. He exchanged a glance with Babineaux, who stroked his moustache and, with a smile flickering on his lips, nonchalantly turned to look up at the fireworks exploding in a dramatic climax above him.

Later, as Annabelle and Mike walked back to the auberge, Mike's phone pinged.

"Huh, looks like we'll be making our own breakfast in the morning. Claude has admitted to sending those poison pen letters. He was warning Father Julien off. Seems like the priest had money problems. He pawned the gold box with the relic of St. Agnès at a shop in Reims. Claude saw him do it."

"Well, well, who would've guessed?"

"Unbelievable." Mike had had his views of the priesthood and those living a religious life shattered in the past few days. He felt like he would never be able to look at a nun in the same way again.

They heard a cry behind them. *"Attendez! Attendez!"* A young mother pushing a child in a buggy ran up to them. She wordlessly pressed a bag into Annabelle's hands. After performing a curious action resembling a curtsey crossed with a bow, the woman ran off again. Annabelle peered into the bag.

"What is it?" Mike said. Annabelle didn't answer. "It's baby clothes again, isn't it?"

"Yes." Annabelle wrinkled her nose at him and smiled coyly. "But let's keep them this time."

EPILOGUE

THERE WAS A slight drizzle as Annabelle's Mini Cooper rolled off the back of the ferry onto British land. The droplets that immediately landed on the car windscreen made Annabelle and Mike smile. They were a subtle reminder that they were home, a final confirmation that the events of the previous week were behind them. And they were a signal that their new lives started now—or at least as soon as they got home.

It was an overcast day, a slight wind picking up the gentle downpour, making it seem more fearsome than it really was. As they drove back to Upton St. Mary, a sense of anticipation and excitement about what awaited came over them.

During their last evening in Ville d'Eauloise, they had learnt that the French were rather good at goodbyes. They took the words *au revoir*—"until we see you again"—literally. Everyone seemed entirely sure that they would meet the English couple again at some point in the future. They had all turned out to greet them on their last evening at

Chez Selwyn, mercifully, in Mike's opinion, leaving the comedy sketch recitals for another time.

"Sometimes," Annabelle said, as she eased the car through the streets towards her church, "I think the best part of a holiday is coming home and appreciating everything you've missed and that you have right at your own front door.

Mike chuckled. "I would agree with that," he said warmly, gently thumbing the lapel of his new coat. "Whilst I enjoyed the pastries and the wine, and the French food, even the snails, what I'm really looking forward to now is a good pie and chips."

Annabelle brought the car to a stop in the church courtyard. They both got out, Mike walking around the car to wrap Annabelle in his arms and plant a loving kiss on her lips.

"Cup of tea?" Annabelle said. "If you're not too eager to get home!"

"I'm already missing you!" Mike said, taking her holdall as they turned to walk up the cottage path. With smiles they couldn't wipe from their faces, they stopped in front of the door, and with a sense of ceremony, Annabelle lifted the large knocker.

After a few moments, the door opened. When Philippa saw who was standing there, she gasped and put her hands to her cheeks. "Oh! You're back!"

"We certainly are," Annabelle said as Magic ran up for some attention. "I know it's my home, but I thought I'd knock rather than surprise you by entering unannounced."

"How lovely to see you. How was it? Was the food as good as they say? Were your rooms warm enough? And what happened with the Catholic business? Did you solve the mystery?" Philippa asked in a rush.

"I'll tell you everything over a cup of tea," Annabelle said.

"Let me go put the kettle on," Philippa replied.

Annabelle and Mike made their way to the living room and stood there listening to Philippa hurriedly clattering teacups and saucers onto a tray.

"We should tell her now," Mike said. "She might spill her tea down herself if we wait."

Annabelle nodded. "Philippa! Would you come in here a moment, please?"

Philippa emerged from the kitchen, her eyebrows high in expectation. "Yes? Is anything the matter?"

"We have some news," Annabelle said, glancing quickly at Mike, who squeezed her waist against his. Annabelle took a deep breath.

Philippa tilted her head, looking back and forth between them. "Yes?"

Annabelle couldn't hold the news in any longer. "Mike proposed!" she said suddenly. "And I said yes! We're getting married!"

Philippa's face went rigid. Her cheeks turned a deep shade of rose-red. She didn't say a word. Annabelle and Mike waited for a reaction, shooting each other a quick, confused glance before looking back at the elderly woman.

"Philippa?" Mike asked. "Are you alright?"

No sooner had he said it than Philippa, stiff as a board, face-planted onto the carpet.

"Oh my!" Annabelle quickly rushed to the fallen woman's side. "Philippa?"

She rolled Philippa onto her back. She slapped her cheeks gently. "Philippa?" Annabelle looked up at Mike. "She's out cold."

Mike crouched down next to her. "Quick, where are your smelling salts?" he said.

"Smelling salts?" Annabelle replied in a panicked tone.

"Yes! Something to bring her back!"

"I haven't got any smelling salts! Who has smelling salts in this day and age?"

"Maybe we should splash some cold water on her?"

"No, too shocking! We might revive her only for her to have a heart attack."

"Well, what then?"

Annabelle gazed down at her friend's pale face with concern. "The holdall!" she said suddenly.

Mike flung the bag open and foraged inside it, tossing aside various garments in search of the carefully wrapped gourmet cheese they had brought back from France. He tore open the soft, waxy covering and rushed to Annabelle's side, breaking off a piece so that she could waft it under Philippa's nose.

"Blurgh!" Philippa said, gasping and smacking her lips as she regained consciousness, shaking her head and paddling the air with her hands as she sought to get herself away from the obnoxious smell.

Mike began laughing. Annabelle joined him. Philippa blinked herself awake.

"Are you alright?" Annabelle asked.

After a short pause during which Philippa looked from Annabelle to Mike, and back again, Philippa smiled and sighed deeply, as though waking from a long, deep, restful sleep. "Did you just say you're getting married?"

"Yes!" Annabelle exclaimed.

Philippa staggered to her feet and hugged both of them with all her tiny might, her eyes glistening with tears. Wordlessly she moved to the coat rack in the hall and put on her hat and her coat. She pulled her brolly from the umbrella stand. Annabelle and Mike looked on in confusion.

"Um . . . Philippa," Mike asked, "what about that tea?"

"Yes," said Annabelle, "we were going to tell you all about our trip!"

"Pfft!" came the older woman's dismissive response. She moved to the door. "I've no time for tea!" She grasped the door handle. "I've got to get on." Philippa turned to look at Annabelle and Mike. "Haven't you heard? I've got a wedding to organise!"

Thank you for reading *Fireworks in France*! I hope you love Annabelle as much as I do. In the next book, *Witches at the Wedding*, will Annabelle and Mike make it down the aisle?

A body in a barn. A secret from the past. Wedding plans can be murder . . .

Reverend Annabelle Dixon is back! A vicar with a taste for sweets and a nose for crime, Annabelle seems doggedly distracted from her impending wedding to Inspector Nicholls. Much to the dismay of her wedding organiser, Philippa.

So when a visiting priest stumbles over a corpse in a cow barn, Annabelle is all too eager to investigate. But when an ancient journal links the victim to a travesty from the past, Annabelle wonders if she's in over her head. Meanwhile, the inspector has his hands full with potential suspects . . . And a troubling lack of clues.

Disgruntled labourers, absent relatives, a group of sinister travellers . . . The list of possible killers seems endless. But when someone burns down Annabelle and Mike's wedding marquee days before the ceremony, they find themselves in a race against time.

Can Annabelle solve this disturbing crime, and banish her wedding day jitters once and for all, before it's too late?

Get your copy of Witches at the Wedding from Amazon to find out! Fireworks in France is FREE in Kindle Unlimited.

To find out about new books, sign up for my newsletter: https://www.alisongolden.com

If you love the Reverend Annabelle series, you'll want to read the *USA Today* bestselling Inspector Graham series featuring a new and unusual detective with a phenomenal memory and a tragic past. The first in the series, *The Case of the Screaming Beauty* is available for purchase from Amazon and FREE in Kindle Unlimited..

And don't miss the Roxy Reinhardt mysteries. Will Roxy triumph after her life falls apart? She's sacked from her job, her boyfriend dumps her, she's out of money. So, on a whim, she goes on the trip of a lifetime to New Orleans, There, she gets mixed up in a Mardi Gras murder. *Things were going to be*

fine. They were, weren't they? Get the first in the series, Mardi Gras Madness from Amazon. Also FREE in Kindle Unlimited!

If you're looking for something edgy and dangerous, root for Diana Hunter as she seeks justice after a devastating crime destroys her family. Start following her journey in this non-stop series of suspense and action. The first book in the series, Snatched is available to buy on Amazon and is FREE in Kindle Unlimited.

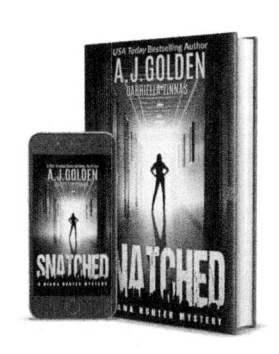

I hugely appreciate your help in spreading the word about *Fireworks in France*, including telling a friend. Reviews help readers find books! Please leave a review on your favourite book site.

Turn the page for an excerpt from the eighth and final book in the Reverend Annabelle Dixon cozy mystery series, *Witches at the Wedding* . . .

A Reverend
Annabelle Dixon
Mystery

witches
at the
wedding

ALISON GOLDEN
JAMIE VOUGEOT

WITCHES AT THE WEDDING
CHAPTER ONE

"THREE DAYS!" PHILIPPA muttered to herself as she plucked a sheet from the washing line and tossed it into the basket beside her. "Only three days left! And she's barely prepared anything!"

Above the rippling, rustling clothes, a pale morning sun cast a gentle glow across Annabelle's cottage. It promised a warm April day. A mild breeze stirred into motion the flowers and shrubs in the pretty cottage garden.

Biscuit, Annabelle's ginger tabby, stalked along the small brick wall that separated the cottage from the fields beyond. She plopped herself down in a sunny spot on top of the wall and stretched out, licking her paws as Magic, Annabelle's dog, scampered around Philippa's feet. The dog was boisterous but wise enough not to get too close to the basket of washing. He knew from experience that Philippa would shoo him away and spoil his fun.

"Does she think the wedding will organise itself?" Philippa picked off the pegs pinning one of Annabelle's clerical undergarments to the washing line and roughly tangled it into a ball. She'd iron it later. Raising her face to the clear blue sky, she closed her eyes, feeling the sun's warmth penetrating her eyelids. "Oh, God, give me strength. I know she's a vicar—one of yours—but she's driving me to distraction. Help me make her see sense."

Philippa continued to toss clothes into the basket, and when the line was empty, Magic still leaping around her, she hoisted the basket onto her hip and stomped towards the cottage. Combining a deft nudge of her toe with the pirouetting skill of a ballerina, Philippa pushed the door open and sidestepped into the cottage, shutting the door with a precisely judged flick of her heel.

"Morning, Philippa," Annabelle said, emerging from the kitchen in a pink bathrobe. She rubbed her wet hair with a towel.

"Morning, Reverend," Philippa said, swallowing her frustration and trapping her thoughts in her mind where they continued to swirl like bees in a jar. She put the basket down beside the ironing board with a bang and shook out a fitted clerical shirt with three-quarter-length sleeves. She whipped it like a sail in a storm. Annabelle took a step back in alarm.

"Goodness, Philippa, you're sharp this morning. Anyone would think you were angry about something." Philippa shook the shirt some more. Annabelle frowned. She liked that shirt. She considered her wrists one of her best features.

Philippa picked up the iron, avoiding Annabelle's gaze. "Have you given any thought to savouries for the reception yet? Sausage rolls or Cornish pasties? We've got plenty of sweets planned." Philippa looked at Annabelle and raised one eyebrow. "But we need to have something for those with different tastes."

Annabelle laughed easily as she moved to the kitchen

counter. "Gosh, no!" she said. "I've just woken up. The only thought on my mind right now is breakfast." It was Philippa's turn to frown, but Annabelle was too busy pouring herself a cup of tea and placing a hot slice of toast on a plate to notice.

On the kitchen table were a host of papers. Annabelle walked over and set her breakfast down. Philippa's frown morphed into wide-eyed horror. Annabelle had placed her tea and toast directly on top of the wedding guest list and meticulous, handwritten notes that Philippa had spent hours poring over. She had laid them on the table for the vicar's inspection.

But it was what Annabelle did next that made Philippa's blood pressure skyrocket. Instead of noticing Philippa's hard work, making a comment, or even perhaps perusing the list of RSVPs, Annabelle blithely grabbed the morning newspaper. She spread it across Philippa's papers before taking a big bite of her toast and leant over to read the headlines!

Philippa's eyes shrunk, her bloodless lips twisted, and her lower jaw was set askew. She became almost unrecognisable. "Unbelievable!" she muttered.

"What's that?" Annabelle said, not looking up as she turned the front page. Philippa gawped at her, incredulous. She involuntarily twitched when Annabelle laughed out loud at something she was reading. The more Annabelle relaxed, the more Philippa's anxiety and frustration grew. She was boiling.

This was too much. Beyond the pale. Philippa opened her mouth, ready to unleash all her irritation, to transgress the boundaries of politeness in a final attempt to shake the vicar into some semblance of sanity with respect to her wedding preparations. But before Philippa could find the words, the morning silence was broken by the sharp tring of the telephone.

"Would you mind getting that, Philippa?" Annabelle mumbled through a mouthful of toast. When Philippa didn't move, Annabelle raised her eyes from her newspaper to gaze at her. "Please."

Philippa clenched her fists, breathed heavily through her nose, and stomped to the telephone. After a brief exchange, she returned to the kitchen. "That was Father John. He's on his way and says he should be here in an hour or two. He says he's looking forward to getting you married."

Annabelle's eyes lit up. "Oh, wonderful! He's rather early though, isn't he? We don't need him until the wedding rehearsal. That isn't until Friday evening."

"Early?" Philippa gasped, her voice high and breathless. Anger coursed through her body, tension that had been increasing for days. "Annabelle," she said, forcing herself to speak calmly. "There's just three more days left to prepare for your wedding. Three days."

Annabelle looked up from her newspaper. She continued to chew on a piece of toast, but her jaw slowed as she considered what Philippa had said. Eventually, she replied. "Yes. I suppose you're right. Do you think Father John will be bored staying so long?"

Philippa squeezed her eyes so tight she saw stars. Her inability to convey the immense gravity of the wedding situation to Annabelle caused her consternation the like of which she hadn't felt since Biscuit brought home a dead rat and dropped it into her cake mix when she wasn't looking.

"Vicar!" Philippa said, marching to Annabelle's side. She leant over to fold the newspaper. "You have three days to coordinate dozens of people so that your wedding occurs without mishap. Three days to ensure your marriage follows the correct protocol of ceremony, reception, and honeymoon, preferably in that order. Three days to ensure all the visitors, guests, and well-wishers, of which there are many, have places to stay, are adequately fed and entertained, and also leave on time, so they don't stay here forever. Three days to finalise the perfect dress, the perfect music, the perfect food, and the perfect vows. Three days to show your future husband what a prize of a bride he has won. Three days to plan and execute the biggest event of your life!"

To get your copy of *Witches at the Wedding* visit the link below:
https://www.alisongolden.com/witches-at-the-wedding

REVERENTIAL RECIPES

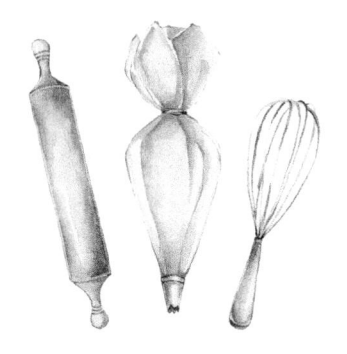

Continue on to check out the recipes for goodies featured in this book...

ANGÉLIQUE APPLE & FIG CHEESECAKE

For the sponge base
2 oz (60g) butter at room temperature
2 oz (60g) self-raising flour, sifted
½ tsp baking powder
1 egg
2 oz (60g) sugar or caster sugar
6 oz (170g) apples, peeled, cored, and sliced
2 oz (60g) figs chopped

For the cheesecake filling
12 oz (340g) fromage frais
3 oz (85g) sugar or caster sugar
½ oz (15g) powdered gelatine
3 tbsp water
1 tsp vanilla extract
One third pint double or whipped cream, whipped
3 egg whites, stiffly whisked

To decorate
1 tbsp sifted icing sugar

3 fl oz (85ml) double or whipped cream, stiffly whipped
A few slices of apples
Chopped figs
Caramel sauce

Preheat the oven to 180°C/350°F/Gas Mark 4. Grease and line a 16cm/7 inch cake tin. Place the butter, flour, baking powder, egg and sugar in a mixing bowl and whisk until light and fluffy. Cook for 20 minutes, Turn out on to a wire tray to cool.

Mix the fromage frais with the caster sugar. Dissolve the gelatine in the water over a gentle heat and add to the cheese with the vanilla extract. Fold in the whipped cream. Lightly fold the whisked egg whites into the cheese mixture.

Lightly oil the sides of a 14cm/6½ inch loose-based cake tin. Cut the sponge in half horizontally and place the bottom half in the tin.

Lay the apples on to the sponge base. Sprinkle the figs evenly over them. Pour in the cheesecake mixture and top with the reserved sponge. Chill until set.

When set, carefully remove from the tin. Dust the top with sifted icing sugar. Decorate with whirls of cream and apple slices and figs. Drizzle with the caramel sauce.

Variations

Cheesecakes make a very versatile dessert with many variations. There are many types of soft cheese now on the market and most are suitable for cheesecakes. Curd cheese, cottage cheese if sieved and skimmed milk soft cheese are all good for keeping the calories down. If full-fat soft cheese is used, half the cream in the recipe can be substituted with plain unsweetened yogurt.

The apples in the recipe can be substituted with any other soft fruit or to make a lemon cheesecake omit the

ANGÉLIQUE APPLE & FIG CHEESECAKE

vanilla essence and add the grated rind and juice of two lemons but add a further ½ teaspoon of powdered gelatine.

If a biscuit crumb base is preferred rather than the sponge base, crumble 6 oz (170g) digestive biscuits or graham crackers, mix with 2 oz (60g) sugar and 2 oz (60g) melted butter. Put half the mixture into the base of the tin then sprinkle the rest over the top.

CHÉRISSABLE CRÈME BRÛLÉE

1 pint (475ml) fresh double or whipping cream
4 egg yolks
3 oz (85g) sugar or caster sugar
1 tsp vanilla extract

Put the cream in the top of a double boiler or in a heatproof bowl over a pan of hot water and bring to just below boiling point.

Meanwhile, put the egg yolks, 2 oz (60g) of the sugar and the vanilla extract in a mixing bowl and beat thoroughly. Pour in the cream and stir to combine. Pour the mixture into a shallow baking dish and place in a roasting tin half full of hot water. Bake in a cool oven 150°C/300°F/Gas Mark 2 for one hour or until set.

When set, remove from the tin and leave to go cold. Chill in the refrigerator for several hours, preferably overnight.

Sprinkle the top of the crème brûlée with the remaining sugar and put under a preheated hot grill until the sugar turns to caramel. Leave to cool before serving.

This sumptuous dessert is at its best served chilled with fresh raspberries or strawberries steeped in vanilla sugar - these contrast well with the richness of the crème brûlée.

DÉLICIEUSE DRIED FRUIT AND SPICE COMPÔTE

4 oz (115g) dried figs
4 oz (115g) dried apricots
2 oz (55g) dried apple
4 oz (115g) dried prunes
2 oz (55g) raisins
2 oz (55g) sultanas
2oz (55g) currants
1 tsp mixed spice
3 tbsp cooking brandy
¼ pint (120ml) strong black coffee
One third pint (160ml) water

This dish is full of nourishment and may be served with a little cream for a lunch or supper dessert or warm it up for comforting breakfast.

Place all the ingredients in a large saucepan and bring gently to the boil. Simmer for 5 - 6 minutes.

Turn the contents of the pan into a large mixing bowl, cover with a clean tea towel, and allow to go quite cold.

Turn the compôte into a large glass or earthenware pot,

seal, and allow to stand in a cool place for at least 12 hours before using.

Note

The compôte may be heated if you wish, but never return any hot leftovers to the main compôte, as all will go bad. If it is properly stored in a cold place, you may add more fruit, cold liquid and brandy (which acts as a preservative). If well sealed, it will keep for more than 2 weeks.

QUALITÉ QUICHE LORRAINE

4-6 oz (115g - 170g) unsmoked streaky bacon, rinds removed and chopped
Shortcrust pastry flan case
2 whole eggs
2 egg yolks
¼ pint (120ml) fresh single cream
Approx. ¼ (120ml) pint milk
Salt and freshly ground black pepper
2 oz (60g) Gruyère cheese, grated

Fry the bacon over gentle heat in a small frying pan until the fat runs and the bacon becomes golden brown. Put the bacon into the flan case.

Beat the whole eggs, egg yolks and cream together lightly in a bowl and pour over the bacon. Stir in enough milk almost to fill the case. Season to taste with salt and pepper and sprinkle with the grated Gruyère.

Bake in a fairly hot oven 190°C/375°F/Gas Mark 5 for 25 to 30 minutes or until the filling is set and the pastry is golden. Remove from the oven and leave to rest for 10 minutes before serving.

SACRÉ STRAWBERRY SOUFFLÉ

¾ lb (340g) fresh strawberries, hulled and washed
5 oz (140g) caster sugar
3 eggs, separated
1 tbsp gelatine powder
2 tbsp lemon juice
Red food colouring (optional)
¼ pint (140ml) fresh double cream
1 oz (30g) finely chopped hazelnuts or walnuts or crushed ratafias to finish

First prepare a 1 pint (475ml) or 13cm/5 inch soufflé dish; cut a strip of doubled greaseproof or baking paper long enough to go around the outside of the soufflé dish (overlapping by 2-5cm/1-2 inches) and 5-7cm/2-3 inches higher than the dish. Tie this securely around the outside of the dish with string. Brush the inside of the greaseproof paper above the rim with melted butter.

Purée the strawberries in an electric blender or work through a sieve, reserving a few whole ones for decoration. Stir in 2 oz (60g) of the sugar.

Put the egg yolks and remaining sugar in a heatproof bowl and stand over a pan of hot water. Beat with a rotary beater or whisk until thick. Remove from the pan and continue beating until the mixture is cold. Fold in the strawberry purée.

Sprinkle the gelatine over the lemon juice in a small heatproof bowl. Leave until spongy, then place the bowl in a pan of hot water and stir over a low heat until the gelatine has dissolved. Leave to cool slightly, then stir into the strawberry mixture. Add a few drops of red food colouring if the mixture seems rather pale. Whip the cream until it is thick and stir into the strawberry mixture, making sure that it is thoroughly blended.

Beat the egg whites until stiff then fold into the strawberry mixture. Spoon into the prepared soufflé dish and chill in the refrigerator for at least 4 hours or until set.

Before serving, carefully remove the greaseproof paper. Decorate the top of the soufflé with the reserved strawberries and press the nuts or ratafias around the edge.

All ingredients are available from your local store or online retailer.

You can find printable versions of these recipes at www.alisongolden.com/ffrecipes

"Your emails seem to come on days when I need to read them because they are so upbeat."
- Linda W -

For a limited time, you can get the first books in each of my series - *Chaos in Cambridge*, *Hunted* (exclusively for subscribers - not available anywhere else), *The Case of the Screaming Beauty*, and *Mardi Gras Madness* - plus updates about new releases, promotions, and other Insider exclusives, by signing up for my mailing list at:

https://www.alisongolden.com/annabelle

TAKE MY QUIZ

What kind of mystery reader are you? Take my thirty second quiz to find out!

https://www.alisongolden.com/quiz

BOOKS IN THE REVEREND ANNABELLE DIXON SERIES

Chaos in Cambridge (Prequel)

Death at the Café

Murder at the Mansion

Body in the Woods

Grave in the Garage

Horror in the Highlands

Killer at the Cult

Fireworks in France

Witches at the Wedding

COLLECTIONS

Books 1-4

Death at the Café

Murder at the Mansion

Body in the Woods

Grave in the Garage

Books 5-7

Horror in the Highlands

Killer at the Cult

Fireworks in France

ALSO BY ALISON GOLDEN

FEATURING INSPECTOR DAVID GRAHAM

The Case of the Screaming Beauty

The Case of the Hidden Flame

The Case of the Fallen Hero

The Case of the Broken Doll

The Case of the Missing Letter

The Case of the Pretty Lady

The Case of the Forsaken Child

The Case of Sampson's Leap

The Case of the Uncommon Witness

FEATURING ROXY REINHARDT

Mardi Gras Madness

New Orleans Nightmare

Louisiana Lies

Cajun Catastrophe

As A. J. Golden
FEATURING DIANA HUNTER

Hunted (Prequel)

Snatched

Stolen

Chopped

Exposed

ABOUT THE AUTHOR

Alison Golden is the *USA Today* bestselling author of the Inspector David Graham mysteries, a traditional British detective series, and two cozy mystery series featuring main characters Reverend Annabelle Dixon and Roxy Reinhardt. As A. J. Golden, she writes the Diana Hunter thriller series.

Alison was raised in Bedfordshire, England. Her aim is to write stories that are designed to entertain, amuse, and calm. Her approach is to combine creative ideas with excellent writing and edit, edit, edit. Alison's mission is simple: To write excellent books that have readers clamouring for more.

Alison is based in the San Francisco Bay Area with her husband and twin sons. She splits her time between London and San Francisco.

For up-to-date promotions and release dates of upcoming books, sign up for the latest news here: https://alisongolden.com/annabelle.

For more information:
www.alisongolden.com
alison@alisongolden.com

- facebook.com/alisongolden.books
- twitter.com/alisonjgolden
- instagram.com/alisonjgolden

THANK YOU

Thank you for taking the time to read *Fireworks in France*. If you enjoyed it, please consider telling your friends or posting a short review. Word of mouth is an author's best friend and very much appreciated.
Thank you,

Printed in Great Britain
by Amazon